For Emma Fagan,
a mighty friend.

Annie   Durinda   Georgia   Jackie

Marcia   Petal   Rebecca   Zinnia

THE Sisters 8

BOOK 8

ZINNIA'S ZANINESS

By Lauren Baratz-Logsted
With Greg Logsted and Jackie Logsted

sandpiper

HOUGHTON MIFFLIN HARCOURT
BOSTON • NEW YORK • 2011

SANDPIPER and the SANDPIPER
logo are trademarks of
Houghton Mifflin Harcourt
Publishing Company.

www.hmhbooks.com

The text of this book is set
in Youbee. Book design by
Carol Chu.

Library of Congress
Cataloging-in-Publication
Data
Baratz-Logsted, Lauren.
Zinnia's zaniness / by
Lauren Baratz-Logsted with
Greg Logsted and Jackie
Logsted.
    p. cm.—(The sisters eight ;
bk. 8) Summary: With the
arrival of August, Zinnia, the
youngest of the Huit octuplets,
eagerly anticipates getting her
power and gift, both of which
hold big surprises that are
revealed to the sisters on their
eighth birthday. [1. Abandoned
children—Fiction. 2. Sisters—
Fiction. 3. Vacations—Fiction.
4. Birthdays—Fiction.
5. Humorous stories.] I. Logsted,
Greg. II. Logsted, Jackie. III.
Title.
PZ7.B22966Zin 2011[Fic]—dc22
2010039257

ISBN 978-0-547-55438-9 paper over board
ISBN 978-0-547-55439-6 paperback

Manufactured in the United States of America • DOC 10 9 8 7 6 5 4 3 •
4500341258

PROLOGUE

Clean my fingernails or don't clean my fingernails? Clean my fingernails or don't clean my fingernails? Clean my—

Oh, hello!

You really are still here, aren't you? It's good to see you, I suppose. And I further suppose you think it's good to see me.

Me.

Me, me, me.

Mi-mi-mi-mi-mi!

Oops, sorry. I just lapsed into song for a moment there, practicing my opera singing. But we weren't talking about *mi,* were we? We were talking about me.

Me.

Now, there's something that's been occupying your mind, hasn't it—the subject of who *I* am. In fact, it's been occupying your mind ever since you first heard about the Sisters Eight, which of course you first heard about from *me.*

You wonder: *Who is that person who keeps talking to us in the prologues?* You wonder: *Are we supposed to know that voice from somewhere?* You wonder: *And does it matter?*

One thing's for certain: I have to be Someone. I mean, I can't be No One, can I? If I were No One, I'd certainly be the most Chatty Cathy of a No One ever.

I'm here to tell you, I'm definitely Someone. In fact — hold on to your hats! — you have already met me in the Sisters Eight books. Well, maybe not *me* in person, as in seeing my face and my body, but you have met my syntax.

Ring any bells yet?

Now, if Jackie were by my side right now, she'd explain that syntax has to do with the way words are put together. So you could say that my personal syntax, not to mention my overall tone, is like a set of fingerprints that give me away. Lots of people have fingers, but no two sets of fingerprints are exactly alike. You can catch a criminal by his or her fingerprints. You'd do well to keep that in mind.

Still not ringing any bells?

Fine. I'll give you one hint:

Dear Rebecca,

I always knew you were a fiery girl —
nice work!

And:

I must say, with you involved, it was always touch and go if this day would ever arrive.

Okay, so maybe that's two hints. So sue me.

Now do you have it? I certainly hope you do. I could give you tons of other examples — well, maybe not tons, but at least a dozen — but honestly, if you haven't figured it out by now . . .

I'm the being the Eights keep referring to as the note leaver.

That's right. Those notes left behind the loose stone in the wall of the drawing room? My handiwork. Mine, all mine. Me.

I suppose now that you know I'm the note leaver, you'd like to know my name too. Isn't that just like people? Give them an inch, they want it all.

Well, we don't have time for that right now because Zinnia's been waiting to have her turn quite long enough. It would be cruel to keep her waiting any longer.

Before I turn the story over to the story, though, I suppose I do need to remind you of the Eights' individual powers and gifts, just in case you've forgotten since last we met.

Annie: power — can think like an adult when
  necessary; gift — purple ring
Durinda: power — can freeze people, except Zinnia;
  gift — green earrings
Georgia: power — can become invisible; gift — gold
  compact
Jackie: power — faster than a speeding train;
  gift — red cape
Marcia: power — x-ray vision; gift — purple cloak
Petal: power — can read people's minds; gift — silver
  charm bracelet
Rebecca: power — can shoot fire from her
  fingertips; gift — a locket

I wonder what Zinnia's power and gift will be. I
wonder if either will prove to be as much of a doozy as
Zinnia has been hoping for. I rather hope so. I have a
certain soft spot for Zinnia.

But there's no time to wonder about that or anything else now because it really is . . .

Zinnia time.

ONE

"Why so glum, chums?" asked Pete.

It was Friday morning, August 1, and we were all hanging around in the drawing room, doing nothing but slouching where we sat, except for Georgia, who was lying on her back on the floor, throwing a ball toward the ceiling and catching it, over and over again. Even the cats were slouching, except for Greatorex, who kept leaping upward in hopes of catching Georgia's ball.

Pete had entered a moment ago with Mrs. Pete. Mrs. Pete had her hair up in curlers while Pete was dressed in his work uniform of a navy blue T-shirt and dangerously low-slung jeans. He had his tool belt on.

We liked Pete's tool belt.

"We are not glum," Annie corrected him. "We are depressed."

"With good cause," Durinda added.

"Okay," Pete said. "Why are you depressed, then?"

"Because it is August," Georgia said, throwing her ball at the ceiling again.

"I don't understand," Pete said. "Isn't that a good thing? August means no more chance of Rebecca shooting fire from her fingertips and perhaps accidentally burning the house down around our ears."

"There is that," Jackie said in an attempt at optimism. But even she couldn't keep that up for very long. She sighed and added, "August seems so very long this year. A whole thirty-one days."

"But that's good, isn't it?" Pete tried again. "You have a whole month of summer vacation left before you go back to school."

"Our birthday is this month," Marcia said. "On August eighth, beginning at eight a.m., we will begin turning eight at the rate of one Eight per minute."

"I did remember that," Pete said. "But isn't *that* a good thing?"

We had to give Pete credit: he did keep trying.

"It is not," Petal said. "For the first time in our lives, Mommy and Daddy will not be with us on our birthday." A tear escaped Petal's eye then, but for once none of us moved to comfort her, not even Durinda or Jackie, because tears were beginning to escape all of our eyes.

"I see," Pete said softly.

"I miss having the ability to shoot fire from my fingertips," Rebecca said. "I know I made a promise not to use that power anymore unless necessary, but I miss just the very idea of that power."

"I thought I would be happy for it to be August," Zinnia said. "It being August means that it is my turn, finally, to get my power and my gift."

"Okay, now I'm sure *that's* a good thing." Pete tried yet again.

We were still willing to give him credit for persistence, but we did think it was time he got a clue gun. He needed to just give up. Couldn't he see that we would not be cheered? That we *could* not be cheered?

"I will be the eighth Eight to get my power and gift," Zinnia said, "after which, according to that first note we found behind the loose stone, we will finally discover what happened to Mommy and Daddy when they disappeared."

"Or died," Rebecca added.

Yes, Rebecca was back to that again. Well, who could blame her for being in a dark mood? We were all in dark moods.

"Now, I know you will try to say that is a good thing, Mr. Pete," Petal said.

We looked at Pete standing there opening his mouth to speak, and we saw that Petal had been right: of course he was about to say that.

"Well, not a good thing if we're talking about what

Rebecca said," Marcia corrected Petal. "Rather, you'll say that what Zinnia said is a good thing."

"The part about finding out what happened to Mommy and Daddy," Jackie said, just so we were all clear. "That's what you'll say is a good thing."

"The problem is," Georgia said, "we are at August first now but August is a whole thirty-one days. Oh, why couldn't August be a shorter month, like June or September? Really, the best thing would be if August were like February, only not during a leap year."

"Georgia's right," Durinda said. Things had to be pretty bad around here if Durinda was agreeing with Georgia. "I think I could bear to wait twenty-eight days to finally learn the truth," Durinda went on. "But waiting thirty-one whole days is really just too much. Then, too, there's always the question *What if the answer is something truly awful?* What will we do then?"

"We usually take a vacation in the summer," Annie said, bringing the conversational ball full circle. We'd begun with Annie and gone one by one down to Zinnia, then back up to Annie again. Sometimes we felt as though our talking was like other people practicing musical scales. "We usually take one in the winter over the holidays and another in the summer. But this summer there won't be one, not without Mommy and Daddy here."

"But what about the trip we took to France?" Pete said.

"That doesn't count as a real vacation," Annie said. "We went there for a wedding, so it was more like a working holiday."

"You could still take a real vacation," a female voice said.

It took us a while to realize who that voice belonged to. We looked around at one another. Nope, that wasn't any of our voices. And it certainly wasn't Pete's. Then we realized it was Mrs. Pete. Pete had been hogging the conversation ball so much, we'd forgotten she was even in the room!

And because it took us a moment to identify the speaker and then another moment to get over our shock at who was actually speaking, it took a further moment for what she'd said to fully register.

"But we can't do that," Georgia objected.

"Of course we can't," Durinda said, once again, shockingly, agreeing with Georgia.

"We can go by ourselves to do a Big Shop," Marcia said.

"Or even a Really Big Shop if necessary," Jackie said.

"But we can't go on a whole vacation all by ourselves," Annie said.

"It is tempting, though," Rebecca said.

"Eight little girls on vacation all by themselves?" Zinnia said. "That would draw too much attention."

"Drawing attention is always a bad thing," Petal

said. "Draw attention to yourself and before you know it, your jig is up. Nope. Sorry. No can do. Perhaps another year. Or better yet, never."

"I meant that we could take you on a vacation," Mrs. Pete said gently.

"We could!" Pete said, taking the conversational ball back from Mrs. Pete. Huh. We'd never noticed before how much more of the talking he did. Maybe it was a guy thing?

Georgia made a face at him. "But don't you have to work for a living?"

"I have read about that," Marcia said. "If a person is supposed to work for a living and he stops doing it for too long, it can be a really bad thing."

"We'd hate to see Bill Collector come after you, Mr. Pete," Petal said solemnly.

Poor Petal. She still believed that all bill collectors were called Bill Collector, even though the only person we'd ever met who was actually named Bill Collector had been very nice to us and hadn't taken any of our money at all.

"I am allowed to take a vacation from time to time," Pete said.

"Seems to me that all you ever do lately," Rebecca said, "is take time off from work."

"I don't think this is really the moment for that, Rebecca," Jackie pointed out. "When the Petes are kind enough to offer to take us on vacation, it hardly seems appropriate to point out Mr. Pete's recent lax work habits."

"I want to go on a vacation!" Zinnia said.

"Oh, I don't know about this," Petal said worriedly. "Don't vacations sometimes end badly for people? If we stay home, we need never find out the answer to that question."

We ignored Petal.

"But if we did go," Annie said, "*where* would we go?"

"Yes," Georgia said, "where? After all, we've already been to Utah, the Big City, and France. What's left?"

The Petes thought about this for a long moment. Well, who could blame them for needing time? It was a tough question. What *was* left?

"The Seaside!" Pete burst out excitedly.

"Oh, I've always wanted to go," Mrs. Pete said.

The Seaside.

Oh, that did sound heavenly.

Suddenly, despite how glum we'd been earlier, we could feel ourselves growing excited. We were daring to hope, daring to dream.

"How would we get there?" Annie asked.

That was Annie all over, we thought, always insisting on being practical.

"I'd suggest my flatbed pickup," Pete said, "but you might get wet if it rains, plus there are no seat belts back there, which is too unsafe for a long road trip, so we'll take your Hummer."

"Thank the universe," Petal said, heaving a little sigh of relief, "that at least *someone* is thinking of safety issues. And thank the universe that we won't be traveling by train or plane. I've had quite enough of those modes of transportation for the time being, thank you very much."

"When would we leave?" Annie said, still being practical.

"Tomorrow," Pete said decisively. "That'll give us today to pack and shop for anything we might need."

"Shopping," Annie mused, "that's good. There are some things I think we should bring with us."

"You mean like sunscreen?" Petal said. "And sunscreen with SPF one hundred for me so that I do not burn to a crisp from the Seaside sun's strong rays?"

"That too," Annie said with a disturbing air of mystery.

What *could* she be thinking of? we wondered.

"And how long will we be gone for?" Annie said, *still* being practical.

"We'll return on August ninth," Pete said, still decisively. "That way we'll be gone from Saturday to Saturday, a good length for any vacation, plus we'll be away from home for your birthday, so you won't have the sadness of celebrating your birthday here without your parents."

This sounded like a good idea to us. If we were somewhere else on our birthday, we wouldn't be constantly looking around the house and envisioning scenes of birthdays past when our parents had been with us. Still, just thinking of spending our birthday *anywhere* without our parents made us sad, so we took a moment to bow our heads.

"So," Pete said, after he'd given us sufficient time for our moment of sadness, "is everyone in agreement? Because we can't go if anyone objects."

"I agree!" Annie said.

"I agree!" Georgia said.

"I agree!" Jackie said.

"I agree!" Marcia said.

"I agree!" Petal said. Then she added, "But with grave reservations."

"I agree!" Rebecca said.

"I *definitely* agree!" Zinnia said.

Mrs. Pete turned to the one non-agreeing Eight. "Durinda?"

"Just who exactly is going to be doing all the cooking on this so-called vacation?" Durinda asked suspiciously.

"We'll go out to eat a lot, I suspect," Pete said. "And if we stay someplace where we have our own kitchen and want to eat in from time to time . . . ?"

"I'll help you, Durinda," Jackie offered.

"We all will," six other Eights also offered.

"That sounds like too many cooks in my kitchen," Durinda said. "Still, I suppose I agree too."

"Yippee!" Zinnia said. "We're going on vacation!"

"But are you really sure you can take so much time off from work?" Rebecca asked Pete. "Won't your boss have some sort of objection?"

Oh, Rebecca.

"I *am* my boss!" Pete was upset. "Why do you think it's called Pete's Repairs and Auto Wrecking? So I think it's safe to say I can give myself the time off without firing me. As for all the cars in the area, they'll just have to refrain from breaking down or needing wrecking while I'm gone."

"Yippee!" Zinnia said. "We're going on vacation!"

"Why don't you all start packing," Annie suggested, "while I go put on my Daddy disguise so I can go shopping and pick up everything we need."

"What about the cats?" Zinnia asked Pete.

Zinnia was referring to Anthrax, Dandruff, Greatorex, Jaguar, Minx, Precious, Rambunctious, and Zither, our eight gray and white puffball cats, one cat per Eight. There was also Old Felix, the Petes' cat, who'd been living with us ever since the Petes temporarily moved in.

"Why, they'll come with us," Pete said. "We can't leave them home alone for a week. I'm sure we can find somewhere to stay that will be happy to have all of us and the cats too."

We weren't sure he should be so sure about that, but we didn't say anything, not wanting to rock the vacation boat.

"Yippee!" Zinnia said. "The cats are going on vacation too!"

We no longer felt glum at all, not even a bit. In fact, as we all hurried to the door so we could begin doing all we needed to do before going away, we were feeling very excited indeed.

"Wait a second," Marcia said, for some reason turning around. "What's that loose stone doing shoving itself a little ways out from the wall?"

We turned.

It was true. The loose stone was jutting out a bit. This, in our experience, could mean only one thing: a new note.

"But that makes no sense," Marcia said. "There should only be a new note if Zinnia has received her power or her gift, neither of which has happened yet."

Marcia crossed the room and angrily pushed the loose stone back into place.

Marcia had had issues with the note leaver ever since Rebecca's month, when we'd discovered Rebecca had superhuman strength but a note to accompany that

never came. Marcia went back and forth now between concern over the note leaver and anger at the note leaver.

"Silly note leaver," Marcia muttered, following the rest of us out of the room.

If she had turned then, if any of us had turned, we would have seen something that we could only have taken as ominous:

The loose stone had already popped itself back out again, as though it were trying to tell us something.

Good thing we didn't turn.

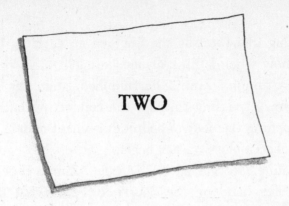

TWO

The next morning found us in our bedrooms putting the finishing touches on our packing.

In bedroom 2, Zinnia looked from Rebecca to Petal to Durinda.

"Rebecca," Zinnia asked, "why are you wearing your locket?"

"Because I always do." Rebecca shrugged. "What's it to you?"

"Petal," Zinnia asked, "why are you wearing your charm bracelet?"

"Because I haven't taken it off since receiving it, not even when I bathe?" Petal asked-answered, as though worried. "Is that the right response?"

"Durinda," Zinnia said, "why are you wearing your dangly earrings with the green stones? And *don't* say because you always do. I know that's not true. They're so fancy, you hardly ever wear them."

"I don't know the right answer," Durinda said,

sounding like Petal as she fingered an earring. "I'll let you know when I think of one."

"Harrumph," Zinnia harrumphed, stomping out of bedroom 2, passing through the connecting bathroom, and opening the door to bedroom 1 with Durinda, Petal, and Rebecca close on her heels.

"Annie, Georgia, Jackie, Marcia," Zinnia said accusingly, her hand on the doorknob, "just what do you think you are doing?"

"What?" Annie, Georgia, Jackie, and Marcia said, looking guilty.

"Annie, you're wearing your purple ring," Zinnia accused. "Georgia, don't bother trying to hide that compact in your hand because I can see the gold glittering between your fingers. Jackie, is there a good reason to pack your red cape for a trip to the Seaside in August?

Marcia, same question for you, only substitute *purple cloak* for *red cape*."

"We're sorry," Jackie said. "Petal thought it wouldn't be safe for us to leave our gifts behind."

"And for once," Georgia said, "we thought the little idiot might be right about something."

"Oh, fine, blame me," Petal said. "Now Zinnia will probably hate me forever and that shall be very bad since Zinnia has always been the kindest to me. Well, except for maybe Durinda. And of course Jackie."

We could tell Annie was a little miffed at being left off Petal's List of Kind People but we were too busy worrying about Zinnia to worry about Annie.

"Didn't it occur to anyone that I might be offended," Zinnia said, "that I might feel *hurt*, since I'm the only Eight without a gift to bring with me on vacation?"

"We're sorry," Durinda said, putting her arm around Zinnia.

"We didn't mean to hurt you," Jackie added, putting her arm around Zinnia from the other side.

"I know!" Annie suggested excitedly in what some of us felt was a thinly disguised attempt to prove she could be as kind as the next Eight. "Why don't you pick something from the house to bring with you — you know, something you personally consider special — so that special something can be your stand-in gift while we're away?"

"Can it be anything?" Zinnia asked.

"Anything," Annie assured her.

A grin as wide as a cape or a cloak spread straight across Zinnia's face.

* * * * * * * *

"Oh no, you are not," Rebecca said, charging down the stairs after Zinnia.

Well, we were all charging at that point.

"Oh yes, I am!" Zinnia shouted gleefully back at us. "Annie said I could bring anything!"

"But I didn't say you could bring *two* anythings!" Annie shouted forward at Zinnia.

"Even I know that if we bring those two . . . *things*," Petal added, "other people will think we are odd."

"And do we really need any more of that in our lives?" Georgia said.

Zinnia reached the bottom of the stairs, which we admit was a very long flight, and headed toward the drawing room, seven Eights in hot pursuit.

That was when Pete blew a whistle.

Oh no. Pete had a whistle. We certainly hoped he didn't plan on blowing it at us a lot while on vacation. That could get annoying.

"Hang on," Pete said, holding one palm up traffic-cop style and causing us to skid to a stop, crashing into each other one by one. "Now, what's all the fuss here?"

Eight Eights spoke at once, so it took a moment for him to sort out what we were saying, but eventually he seemed to get the idea.

"Let me see if I've got this straight," Pete said as

Mrs. Pete came over to join him. "Seven of you are bringing your special gifts on vacation because you're worried they'll get stolen if you leave them home. Zinnia's upset because she doesn't have a special gift to bring. Annie said she could take along whatever she wanted from the house to be her stand-in gift until the real thing comes along. Zinnia wants to bring that suit of armor and dressmaker's dummy that you lot refer to as Daddy Sparky and Mommy Sally."

It was true, we had to admit with embarrassment. Zinnia *did* want to take the suit of armor and the dressmaker's dummy on vacation with us. Could she *be* any zanier?

"And now," Pete said in conclusion, "Petal, of all people — sorry, Petal, but I think you understand — *Petal,* the same Petal who hid under beds in not one but two different countries for the better part of the month of June, is concerned that other people might think you lot are odd?"

Eight heads nodded.

"I'm sorry to have to be the one to tell you this," Pete said, "but that ship has already sailed."

"He means that everyone already thinks we're odd," Jackie said.

"There was no need to translate, Jackie," Annie said. "We were all able to figure out that figure of speech on our own."

"I wasn't," Petal said.

"Does this mean that it's okay with you, Mr. Pete," Zinnia asked, "if Daddy Sparky and Mommy Sally come along for the ride?"

"I don't see why not," Pete said.

"Phew," Zinnia said.

Even though we'd never have admitted it out loud, we shared Zinnia's *phew*. The Petes were great, but since New Year's Eve, we'd grown kind of used to having Daddy Sparky and Mommy Sally as our stand-in parents. They may not have been big talkers, and their versions of hugs did leave something to be desired, but we had missed them when we went to France—you simply can't take a suit of armor on an airplane with you, what with all those metal detectors, plus we couldn't possibly split up Daddy Sparky and Mommy Sally—and we would have missed them if we had to leave them a second time.

"But if Daddy Sparky and Mommy Sally are with us," Petal worried aloud, "and we're all gone too, plus the cats, who will keep an eye on the house? You can't leave a house behind with no one to keep an eye on it. It's unsafe!"

"People usually ask their neighbors to keep an eye out," Durinda said.

"Somehow," Annie said, "I don't think asking the Wicket to do that is such a good idea."

Did we really need her to tell us that?

"What about Carl the talking refrigerator and robot Betty?" Pete suggested.

"Haven't you noticed," Georgia said, "that Carl's a talking refrigerator but not a walking refrigerator? If someone bad breaks in, what can he do? Toss ice cubes at them? He certainly can't chase them anywhere."

"Haven't you noticed," Rebecca added, "that robot Betty never follows instructions? Tell her to keep all the riffraff out, you know she'll just go watch TV."

"Since Carl the talking refrigerator and robot Betty won't do us any good if we leave them behind," Petal said, "can we take them with us this time?"

We ignored Petal.

"I'm sure everything will be just fine here," Pete said.

"Can we go get Daddy Sparky and Mommy Sally from the drawing room," Zinnia asked, "so we can begin loading them and everything else into the car?"

Zinnia didn't wait for an answer.

And as the rest of us followed her into the drawing room, we saw that the loose stone was once again sticking out.

"Silly note leaver," Marcia muttered, shoving the stone back in again.

"Stop doing that," Zinnia said, upset. "It's my month.

I should be in charge of shoving the loose stone back in if it needs it."

Just as Zinnia finished her last sentence, the stone popped out again.

Marcia reached to shove it back in but Zinnia stopped her just in time.

"I *said*," Zinnia said with rare forcefulness, "that's *my* job this month."

Then Zinnia reached for the stone, but instead of shoving it back in again, she slid it the rest of the way out.

"Well, what do you know?" Zinnia said, peering into the space where the stone had been. "There *is* a note back here."

We all gathered round as Zinnia pulled out the note and began to read:

Dear Zinnia,

It seems I've been waiting to say this to you for far too long: Congratulations on your magnificent power!

Of course, I did try to congratulate you yesterday, at the earliest possible moment of your official month, but <u>someone</u> shoved the stone back in. So I was forced to congratulate you today instead.

Fifteen down, one to go. I do hope you've been enjoying your power. I hope you agree that it is, as you would say, a doozy!

As always, the note was unsigned.

We did think that it would be nice if, just once, the note leaver forgot about not signing his or her — or its — name, and went ahead and signed it. Who could this person be?

"I don't understand this," Marcia said, frustrated.

"This is ridiculous," Rebecca said. "Zinnia hasn't received any power."

"Maybe I have," Zinnia said in a small voice.

"That's crazy talk," Georgia said. "Can you think like an adult?"

"I don't know how I'd know if I could do that," Zinnia said, "but I'm fairly certain I can't."

"Can you make other people freeze?" Annie asked.

Zinnia tried rapidly hitting her palm against her leg and then pointing at various ones of us but none of us froze.

"No," Zinnia said, "nor can anyone freeze me."

"Can you make yourself disappear?" Durinda asked.

Zinnia twitched her nose twice. "Can you still see me?" she asked hopefully.

" 'Fraid so," Durinda said.

"Then I guess the answer must be no," Zinnia said sadly.

"Can you run faster than a speeding train?" Marcia asked.

"Do you have one handy?" Zinnia asked. Then, not waiting for a response, she added, "I'm sure I can't, even if you did."

"Do you have x-ray vision?" Jackie asked.

Zinnia squinched her eyes tight. "No," she said.

"Good," Petal said. "That means you can't see my underwear."

"Can you read people's minds?" Rebecca asked.

"No," Zinnia said, "but I can guess what you're thinking about me and I know it's not good. And before you ask, no, I can't shoot fire from my fingertips."

"Then what *can* you do?" Georgia demanded.

"I can talk to the cats," Zinnia said simply. "I can understand them and they can understand me." She shrugged. "It's the same power I've had all my life."

"That's not a power," Georgia said, laughing in her face. "That's just your insanity."

One day we would regret doing it, but in that moment, we laughed at Zinnia too.

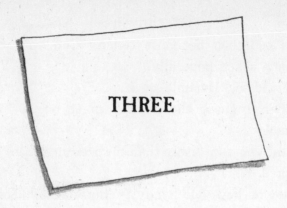

THREE

"Let's pack up the car so we can hit the road!" seven of us cried with great enthusiasm and one of us cried with half enthusiasm. That half enthusiast would be Zinnia, who, we suspected, still felt bad that we'd laughed at her. But we weren't worried. She'd get over it. She always did.

"I've got the packing manifest here," Annie said, pulling out a pen and clipboard to which she'd attached a sheet of paper.

"Must we have a packing manifest?" Georgia groaned.

"Can't we just pack the car without one, like normal people?" Rebecca added.

"I don't even know what a manifest is," Petal said. "Will it hurt, like getting a shot at the doctor's office?"

"No," Jackie reassured her. "A *manifest* in the way Annie's using it is simply a fancy name for a list."

Annie stood beside Mrs. Pete, checking off items on her list as Pete loaded the purple Hummer.

"Ten suitcases?" Annie called to Pete.

"Check!" he called back.

"The big bag we'll take to the beach with items like regular sunscreen for the rest of us and SPF one hundred for Petal?" Annie called.

"Check!" Pete called back.

"Snacks for the ride?" Annie called.

"Check!" Pete called back.

"How long will the ride be?" Petal asked.

We ignored her.

"Our eight cats plus Old Felix and all the cat things?" Annie called.

"Check!" Pete called back.

"Daddy Sparky and Mommy Sally?" Annie called.

"Check!" Pete called back. He sounded like he might be getting tired and out of breath. We hadn't known that could happen to Pete. "Are we almost finished with your manifest, Annie?" he asked. "It's getting a little cramped in there. I'm not sure there will be room for all of us humans if you try to cram any more stuff in."

"That's okay," Annie said, "because there's just one box left."

"A box?" Pete looked surprised, and then he saw Annie point to a box near her feet. "What's in that box?" he wanted to know. "I don't remember seeing the word *box* anywhere on your manifest."

"Oh, it's just something we Eights need to take on

vacation with us," Annie said with that disturbing air of mystery again.

"Oof!" Pete said, lifting the box off the ground. "This box is heavy. What have you got in here, old books?"

"Never mind that now," Annie said as Pete crammed that one last item into the Hummer. "We need to go say goodbye to Carl the talking refrigerator and robot Betty."

* * * * * * * *

Clink, clink, clink.

The ice-cube dispenser was making rapid clinking noises, which in our house could mean only one thing: the talking refrigerator was crying.

"Stop crying, Carl," Durinda said. "We'll come back."

"Don't forget to eat proper meals while you're away from me," Carl the talking refrigerator said morosely.

Clink, clink.

"We won't," Durinda assured him, spreading her arms wide to give him a hug.

"Just because it's summer," Carl said, "doesn't mean you can eat ice cream all day long."

"We know that, Carl," Durinda said.

"But I *will* keep the ice cream at home perfectly chilled for your return," Carl said.

Clink.

"We know that too, Carl," Durinda said. "You always take such good care of us."

"Durinda," Rebecca said, "do you think you could stop hugging the talking refrigerator already so we could leave on our vacation?"

"Oops, sorry," Durinda said with a blush as she forced herself away from Carl. "I hadn't realized I was still doing that."

"Goodbye, Carl!" we all shouted as we headed for the door.

"Goodbye, Betty!" we all shouted as we passed her on our way out the door. "Take good care of Carl for us!"

The robot slammed the door behind us.

It was anyone's guess what the robot would do with us gone.

But at that moment, all we were thinking was *Yippee! Vacation time!*

* * * * * * * *

"One hundred boxes of juice on the wall, one hundred boxes of juice! You take one down, pass it around, ninety-nine boxes of juice on the wall!"

Big breath.

"Ninety-nine boxes of juice on the wall, ninety-nine bo—"

"Excuse me," Pete said, interrupting our singing, which we'd decided to take random turns at so that no one's voice gave out before the end of the song, "but why do you say 'boxes of juice'?"

"What else would we say?" Jackie asked.

"Well," Marcia said, "I believe in the original song, it's 'bottles of beer.'"

"We can't sing about bottles of beer," Petal said. "We're kids. We could get arrested for that."

"That's not what I meant," Pete said.

"Then why don't you say what you meant so that we'll all know?" Rebecca said.

Oh, Rebecca.

Near the end of July we'd grown hopeful about Rebecca. She'd seemed so much more mature, nicer even.

But that hadn't lasted. That had been our experience with most people: they changed very little or, if they did change a lot, they soon went back to the way they'd been before the changing. Now Rebecca was pretty much back to being Rebecca, which meant awful. Oh, well. At least she wasn't using her superhuman strength to do any of us grievous bodily harm. We figured we would take what we could get.

"It's just that I happen to know that your favorite flavor of juice is mango," Pete said.

"I prefer just plain glasses of pulp," Rebecca said.

We ignored her.

"So I guess what I was wondering was," Pete said, "why don't you sing 'One hundred boxes of mango juice on the wall, one hundred,' and so on and so forth?"

"Who was doing the singing when we got interrupted?" Georgia said.

"I was," Durinda said. "I was doing ninety-nine."

"Please sing Mr. Pete's version," Annie said, "so he can see."

"Perhaps I'd better start at the beginning," Durinda said. "I seem to have forgotten where I left off."

"Just do it!" Rebecca shouted.

Do you see what we mean about Rebecca?

"Ninety-nine boxes of mango juice on the wall, ninety-nine boxes of mango juice! You take one down, pass it around, ninety-eight boxes of mango juice on the wall!"

"Do you see now, Mr. Pete?" Jackie asked gently.

"No," Pete said. "I see nothing except for the road in front of me. Oops! Train crossing!"

Whoa, that was close.

"Don't even bother, girls," Mrs. Pete said as the train finished crossing our path and we were safe to drive over the railroad tracks. "He's always been like this."

"I've always been like what?" Pete said, sounding offended.

"I hate to say it," Mrs. Pete said, "but you don't really have any rhythm."

"I'm afraid she's right, Mr. Pete," Marcia said. "The two syllables that the word *mango* adds throw off the entire rhythm of the song."

Pete hummed quietly to himself for a time before bursting out with "I do believe you're right — I've got no rhythm!"

* * * * * * * *

"Fifty-three boxes of juice on the wall, fifty-three boxes of juice! You take one down, pass it around, fifty-two boxes of juice on the wall!"

"Nice singing, Zinnia," Annie said. "Who wants to go next?"

"How long have we been driving?" Petal asked.

Judging from the changes in the sky, at least a few hours had passed since we'd left home, but we didn't say that because Petal might worry we'd been driving so long our car would fall off the edge of the Earth.

We hate to admit it, but we were fairly certain there were moments Petal believed the Earth was flat.

"How long until we get there?" Petal asked.

We ignored this question too because we didn't know the answer. Who knew how long it would take us to get where we were going? We certainly hoped we didn't run out of song first.

"Fine," Petal said, and we realized that the realization that we were going to go on ignoring her questions must have sunk in. "I'll do fifty-two. I'm only glad those are boxes of juice and not bottles. With all of them practically falling off the wall like that, what if one fell on my head? I could get crushed! Although I suppose that one hundred boxes of juice, were they all to fall on my head at once, could kill me just as neatly as one well-placed bottle."

"The song isn't about falling objects!" Georgia said, exasperated. "It's just about taking drinkable items off the wall!"

"Well, but they could fall," Petal said, "and if they did, they could be deadly, so—"

"Never mind," Jackie said, cutting Petal off with a gentle pat on the arm. "I'll take fifty-two."

"Twenty-seven boxes of juice on the wall—"

"Oh, this drive is going by so quickly," Zinnia said with breathless wonder as the pretty world zipped past our window. "Whoever invented this song is a genius!"

* * * * * * *

"One box—"

"We're here!" Pete announced joyfully, pulling up at the Seaside.

"Hey!" Rebecca was outraged. "That was my turn you just cut off!"

We ignored her.

While ignoring Rebecca, we all piled out of the car to stretch our legs after the long trip. We'd left sometime in the morning and now it was nearly dark out: royal purple, midnight blue, and just a single sliver of gold streaking the sky.

How long had we been on the road?

How long had we been singing that song?

"I'll tell you one thing," Mrs. Pete said, "Zinnia's right. Whoever invented that song is a genius. Why, it kept us happily busy the whole trip!"

"Fine for you to say," Pete said. "You've got rhythm."

"Don't worry, Mr. Pete," Jackie said. "You've got plenty of other good qualities."

"Thanks, pet," Pete said.

"I wonder," Marcia said, "if that song is expandable."

We were too tired after all that time in the car to even ask her what she was talking about, and some of us were even too tired to mock her, so we simply stood there, waiting for her to get on with it.

"It took us right up to the last box of juice in the song to arrive at our destination," Marcia said. "But what if our trip had lasted twice as long? What if it had been half as short? Would that one song last us exactly the entire trip, no matter how long or short the trip might be?"

Even Pete, who was usually polite about Marcia's peculiar displays of her peculiar brand of intelligence, saw fit to ignore that.

"I'll just go see," Pete said, eyeing the long array of hotels, motels, and other touristy-looking places that lined the Seaside, "about getting lodging for us all for the night."

One place that would take all of us? He'd said something about this earlier. We hadn't commented at the time, and we certainly weren't about to comment now, except perhaps to say to ourselves, very quietly: "Oh, Mr. Pete. What can you possibly be thinking?"

One place fitting all? As if.

As if!

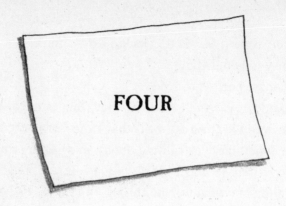

FOUR

"We'll leave all our things in the car while we go find a room," Pete said, "and then we'll come back for them."

Ah, a man with a plan.

"Don't you mean three rooms, Mr. Pete?" Marcia asked him.

"A fourth room for the cats would be nice," Zinnia added. "We don't mind being split up into four and four, but the cats rather prefer to stay all together."

All of us ignored Marcia and Zinnia, including Pete, who probably hadn't planned on springing for an extra room for the week just for the cats.

We set off walking along the boardwalk, looking for a place where we might like to stay. Other people were walking along the boardwalk too, whole families looking happy together. The night air was filled with the sounds of laughter and the smell of cotton candy, and it was all very exciting.

"'The Big Hotel.'" Pete read the large neon sign at the place where we'd stopped. "This looks promising, since we're such a big group."

We strolled into the lobby, which was very big indeed, and then strolled all the way up to the registration desk.

"Welcome to the Big Hotel," the man behind the desk said. "How may I help you?"

"Do you have any rooms available?" Pete asked.

"We do indeed," the man said. "How many will you need?"

"Three," Pete said.

"Four," Zinnia corrected him. "I thought we agreed about the cats."

"I really do think three will be sufficient," Pete said.

"Back up a minute," the man said. "Did you say *cats?*"

Before we could answer, the man stretched across the desk and looked down. He caught sight of eight girls and nine cats, and shock filled his eyes. How had he not noticed us before? we wondered. The man straightened up again.

"I'm sorry, sir," the man said abruptly to Pete, "but there's been a mistake. There are no rooms available here. Please try another hotel."

Pete looked surprised at this sudden turn of events. We suspected he was the only one who was. Not only did Mrs. Pete have all the rhythm, she also had more than her share of common sense.

"I see," Pete said to the man, even though, clearly, he didn't. "Where do you suggest I try?"

The man pointed his finger toward the door that would take us back out to the boardwalk and then hooked his finger to the left. "Try thataway," he said.

"Who says *thataway*?" Rebecca muttered as we headed toward the door. "Where does he think he is, in the middle of a Western?"

Back outside into the boardwalk-strolling throngs, we headed thataway, trying each hotel we came to, all with the same result.

"How about this?" Pete suggested. "The Medium Hotel."

"I wonder if the name refers to the hotel's size," Jackie said, "or that it specifically caters to people who think they can talk to the dead."

"I don't think I want to stay here," Petal said. "It sounds too scary."

We ignored Petal.

And the lady behind the registration desk ignored us when she saw how big a group we were.

"Huh," Pete said, confused as we exited yet an-other hotel. "I guess people around here don't need our business. You'd think any hotel would be happy to have us."

No, Mr. Pete, we thought, *only* you *would think that.*

The thing was, when our parents were still with us, we'd stayed at hotels from time to time, and we already knew what Pete was only just discovering: no one was ever *happy* to have us.

Back on the boardwalk, Pete looked left and right dejectedly. "Which way now?" he asked.

"How about thataway?" Rebecca said.

So we went thataway and we kept on going thataway until we came to . . .

"The Little Hotel," Pete said. "Look at this puny place, all rundown. Surely it could use our business."

Surely it could not.

The man behind the little registration desk didn't even wait for Pete to ask if there were any rooms available. He simply laughed in our faces.

"I take it the answer is no?" Pete said to the man, who just kept on laughing. "Is it because of the cats?" Pete persisted.

"That too," the man said, looking at us Eights and laughing some more.

Since when were we something to be laughed at? We must say, we were very offended.

"Maybe," Georgia said, "instead of trying places that cater to people who think they can talk to the dead or places that don't seem to want to make any money off us, we should look for a place that caters to people who think they can talk to cats. That way Zinnia could get us in."

The man studied Zinnia with new interest. "Could you talk to my cat?" the man asked. "Orange hasn't been eating lately and I'm worried she might be sick."

Orange. Seven of us laughed. What a silly name for a cat.

"I can try," Zinnia said, ignoring us. "But you mustn't expect too much. If Orange is just meeting me, she might be shy about confessing her deepest, darkest secrets."

The man brought out Orange, who was black, which we agreed made absolutely no sense at all, and set her on the registration desk.

"Can you give me a boost up, Mr. Pete?" Zinnia asked.

Sometimes we forgot how small Zinnia was. In addition to each of us being born a minute apart, with Annie the oldest, each of us was an inch shorter than the previous sister, with Annie the tallest. This meant that Zinnia was a full seven inches shorter than Annie, making Zinnia very short indeed.

Pete did the boosting, and Zinnia and Orange commenced their Eight-to-cat conversation. There was a lot of Zinnia whispering in Orange's furry ear and then Orange doing something that looked like whispering in Zinnia's nonfurry ear.

Occasionally, like now, we were impressed with

Zinnia. What a show she was capable of putting on! A person might almost believe she *could* talk with cats!

Of course, Rebecca would have us change that: *a crazy* person might almost believe that.

Zinnia wrapped up her end of the whispering and told Pete he could stop boosting her. Then she looked up at the man.

"Orange says she is sick," Zinnia said, hurrying to add, "but only in that she is sick of the brand of kibble you've been feeding her. Orange says she wishes you would buy Kitten Kaboodle, the brand with the picture of happy cats on the bag that they're always advertising during the late-late-late movie on channel three-twelve. Orange says the other cats on the boardwalk say it's the best, much better than that cheap Kibble Kan't you've been feeding her."

The man looked embarrassed. "I wasn't meaning to be cheap," he said. "I always thought the cats on the Kibble Kan't bags looked happy enough."

"Not as happy as the Kitten Kaboodle cats," Zinnia insisted. She turned to Jackie. "Jackie, could you run to the car and get the bag of kibble we brought to feed the cats?"

Jackie got the keys from Pete and took off running.

"Jackie's the fastest among us," Durinda explained to the man.

And Jackie proved it, returning very rapidly with the large bag of kibble.

"Do you see now?" Zinnia said to the man as she pointed to the cats on the bag.

The man saw. We all saw.

Zinnia was right: those were some *insanely* happy cats.

"Do you have Orange's kibble bowl handy?" Zinnia asked the man.

"Since she's so fast," the man said, "can I send — what was her name? Jackie? — to go fetch it?"

We just stared at him. How would Jackie know where he kept his cat's kibble bowl?

"I was kidding," he finally said. "Back in a tick."

It was more like a tick *and* a tock — he was no Jackie, after all — but soon he was back with the requested bowl into which Zinnia poured a large serving of Kitten Kaboodle.

Our eight cats plus Old Felix looked at Zinnia like she was crazy to give so much of the good stuff away.

"Don't worry," Zinnia assured them. "There's plenty for everybody."

Orange devoured the Kitten Kaboodle so fast, she was licking her chops in no time.

"As you can see," Zinnia told the man, "Orange is *not* sick."

"She just didn't like the lousy cheap food you were giving her," Georgia added.

"Now that Zinnia has solved your cat problem," Mrs. Pete said, "do you think you might be able to find rooms for us?"

We laughed at the idea of Zinnia solving the man's cat problem. Of course Zinnia hadn't had a conversation with Orange. That whole thing with Kitten Kaboodle was just a lucky guess!

Some of us were getting tired, however. So if Zinnia's lucky guess could get us a room, or three, or four . . .

But the man just laughed in our faces again.

How offensive! And after what Zinnia had done for him. Still, as we watched Rebecca, who'd grown bored and was now playing one-person catch in the tiny lobby using Petal as a human ball, we couldn't say that we blamed him. We were a lot to handle.

But something in our expressions as we turned away from the desk must have caused him to take pity on us.

"Wait," he said. "You still can't stay here, and I can't think of any self-respecting establishment that would have you. But there's a house you might be able to rent for the week."

"A house, you say?" Pete's expression was happy again as we turned to face the man.

"We don't want a house," Georgia said. "We already live in one of those. This is vacation. We want to stay somewhere special."

Oh, Georgia.

"That's fine, that's fine," the man said hurriedly. "It's more of a cottage anyway, but there should be room for all of you. It's all the way at the end of the beach. Goes by the name of the Last-Ditch Cottage. I'm sure no one's using it this week. Almost no one ever does."

"Is it haunted?" Petal asked fearfully.

We ignored Petal, but the man didn't.

"No," he said. Then he shrugged. "Last-Ditch just isn't what most people usually have in mind when they go on vacation."

"It sounds perfect for us, then," Pete said.

Poor Pete. He was finally getting the picture. We weren't "most people."

"Who do I talk to about renting it?" Pete asked.

"You mean right now?" the man asked.

"No, he means next year," Rebecca said. She tossed Petal again before adding in exasperation, "Of course he means now."

Rebecca was being rude, we thought, but she did have a point.

"Oh, it's much too late right now," the man said. "I know a man who knows the man who rents it. Come back in the morning and I'll have the key and the paperwork for you."

"And where do you suggest we sleep until morning?" Mrs. Pete wanted to know.

"I don't know." The man shrugged. "Maybe on the beach?"

* * * * * * * *

Okay, so there were no rooms for us at the inns and maybe we were roughing it more than we were accustomed to, but it was rather cozy on the beach at night, nestled into the sand dunes, with what seemed like a million stars twinkling overhead.

"I hope it doesn't rain," Petal said.

"There's not a cloud in the sky," Pete said.

"I hope we don't get hit by a tidal wave," Petal said.

"I'm sure they don't have those here," Mrs. Pete said.

"Oh, look!" Jackie said. "A shooting star!"

We all looked. How dazzling!

"Quick, make wishes, girls," Mrs. Pete said. "That's what you do when you see a shooting star."

We were grateful she was there to tell us that. We'd never seen a shooting star before and so we didn't know what to do with one, other than be dazzled by it.

"I wish we had that box with us now," Annie said. "Too bad we left it in the car."

"I wish for real French potatoes so that someday I can make real French fries," Durinda said.

"I wish for a bed," Georgia said, "because this sand is lumpy."

"I wish for Georgia to stop complaining," Jackie said, "and to just be happy with wherever she is at the moment, for her sake, not ours."

"I wish for even greater math skills than I already possess," Marcia said.

"I wish to not be scared of everything," Petal said, "and not to die."

"I wish I had a can of pink frosting," Rebecca said.

"I wish it were September already," Zinnia said, "because even though that would mean that my month was over with, my moment in the spotlight history, maybe somehow Mommy and Daddy would be back with us again."

We were all silent for a minute, thinking how much better Zinnia's wish was than any of ours.

Then:

"Oh no! Not a shooting star!" Petal shrieked. "You mean the sky is shooting at us?"

Then she buried her head in the sand.

"Maybe we should just do our Waltons routine and then go to sleep?" Annie suggested with a weary sigh.

Our Waltons routine was something we got from an old TV show. At the end of each episode, the members of the large family each randomly called out good nights to one another.

So that's what we did. We spent a half-hour saying our good nights and then we went to sleep.

FIVE

The next morning found us up bright and early. We grabbed a quick breakfast on the boardwalk before heading back to the Little Hotel.

"Just sign this paperwork," the man told Pete, "and then I can give you the key."

So Pete did, and the man did, and then we were back in the Hummer, driving all the way to the very end of the beach, where we saw . . .

"I see why it's called the Last-Ditch," Pete said.

"It looks more like a shack than a cottage," Georgia said.

"It's so dingy and gray," Marcia observed.

"It looks like a stiff wind could blow it over," Durinda said.

"Do you think that roof is safe?" Petal worried out loud.

For once we didn't feel that Petal was off base in

being worried. That roof looked like someone had put it on with a cheap stapler.

"I'm sure this will be fine," Pete said as we approached the door, which was at an angle on its hinges.

"Huh," he said as we stepped onto the creaky porch. "It looks like there's a folded piece of paper taped to the door."

"I don't know why there should be a piece of paper there," Annie said. "Didn't you already sign all the paperwork on this place back at the Little Hotel?"

Pete didn't answer. Instead, he untaped the piece of paper and unfolded it.

"Huh," he said again, then he handed the paper to Zinnia. "It's for you."

Zinnia read the note out loud.

Dear Zinnia,

Have I said it yet today? Congratulations on your doozy of a power!

"I can't believe this," Jackie said. "No matter where we are—at home, on a plane over the ocean, here—somehow the note leaver finds us!"

"What I can't believe," Marcia said, grabbing the note from Zinnia's hand and crumpling it into a ball, "is how unreliable the note leaver has become. First the note leaver had no knowledge of Rebecca's superhuman strength, and now the note leaver keeps talking about Zinnia's power when clearly she has none. It's just too much."

"Hey!" Zinnia yelled. "That note was my property!"

All of a sudden, something flew over our heads.

"Hey!" Durinda said. "A carrier pigeon!"

Carrier pigeons often delivered notes to us when we were at home, but it had been quite some time since we'd seen one and we'd certainly never seen one when we *weren't* at home.

Usually when carrier pigeons visited us at home, they went straight to Durinda. Well, perhaps it was because she was almost always the one to open the window and let them inside. But not this time. This time, the carrier pigeon went to Zinnia, landing on her shoulder.

Zinnia turned her head a bit so that she and the carrier pigeon were eye to eye.

"Hello," Zinnia said out loud.

This was odd; usually when Zinnia pretended she could talk to one of our cats, she did so in a whisper.

The carrier pigeon made some sort of noise.

"That's funny," Marcia said. "I didn't think carrier pigeons could talk."

"That's because they can't," Georgia said.

"Better watch it," Rebecca warned Marcia, "or Georgia will start calling you 'you little idiot' too."

"Do you have a name?" Zinnia asked the pigeon.

The pigeon made another sound.

"Did it say Caw?" Annie asked.

"Or was that Kaw?" Jackie suggested.

"Call," Zinnia said. "I see. C'mon, Call, let's go in the cottage."

"Are you going to let her keep that?" Rebecca asked Pete.

"I don't see why not." Pete shrugged. "Besides, we have bigger things to worry about right now, like unpacking all our gear from the car and then getting settled in our new surroundings."

"*New* surroundings," Georgia scoffed softly as we followed Zinnia over the threshold. "More like *old and shabby* surroundings."

Georgia was right for once. The cottage was old and shabby, with dust and cobwebs everywhere, musty sheets covering the furniture.

"Aren't you worried the cats will eat your new pet?" Rebecca asked Zinnia.

"Call's not a pet, it's a friend," Zinnia corrected. "And no. The cats have promised they will not."

We rolled our eyes.

"I knew Annie should have let me buy that birdcage at the store that time," Petal said. "I don't think it's safe to have a pigeon just flying loose indoors willy-nilly."

"C'mon, Call," Zinnia said. "Let's go see the rest of the place."

"I suppose we should be grateful Zinnia didn't name it C'mon," Georgia said. "That would get so annoying."

"Confusing too," Petal added, "because we'd never know who she was talking to any time she said 'C'mon, C'mon' — one of us or the bird."

"No," Rebecca said. "It would just be annoying."

"Hey," Zinnia said to the pigeon as we investigated the room we guessed was supposed to be the living room given its view of the ocean through grimy windows, "did you bring that note for me?"

What a silly question. What did Zinnia think, that the pigeon had come equipped with tape in order to tape her note to the door?

And why was she still talking aloud to it? Was she trying to demonstrate for us her power — you know, the power we all knew she didn't possess?

"Who sent you?" Zinnia asked the pigeon.

The pigeon made a sound. Whatever Zinnia thought that sound meant, it caused her to look confused and then glance around at us.

"That's odd," she said. "Call answered my question by saying 'Zinn.' But that makes no sense. Zinn is the first syllable in my name, and I know *I* didn't send the pigeon to me."

"Maybe Call is just confused," Jackie said kindly. "When the carrier pigeons visit us at home, sometimes they strike their bodies against a window to get attention. Maybe Call accidentally struck its head."

Oh, Jackie, we thought. It's one thing to be kind, but did she really need to go to such great lengths to humor the loony?

"Why don't we go to the kitchen, Call," Zinnia suggested, "and get you a nice cool drink of water?"

"Oh no!" Durinda cried. "Does this place have a . . . *kitchen?*"

"Well," Pete said, looking embarrassed, "you know, it is a cottage, not a hotel, and the man back at the Little Hotel did say something about —"

"Why don't you see if there are any supplies in the kitchen," Rebecca told Durinda. "I'm feeling a bit peckish." She cracked her knuckles. "Still gotta keep my strength up, you know."

"I'm feeling hungry too," Georgia added. "Do you think the previous renters left fixings for chocolate chip pancakes?"

"Perhaps after we unpack and spend a few hours on the beach," Pete said, "I should find a grocery store so we can stock up."

"I *knew* this vacation would somehow result in my cooking!" Durinda fumed.

* * * * * * * *

Once we de-fumed Durinda with promises to help her—it was anyone's guess if we would keep our promises—we set about the business of unpacking the car. Once again, Annie had a clipboard with a manifest attached, this time an unpacking manifest.

"Mr. Pete," Annie directed, "you bring your and Mrs. Pete's suitcases to the biggest bedroom."

"Thanks, pet," Pete said. "It's nice of you to assign us the biggest room."

"Not really," Annie said. "It's just that there's only one biggest room. If one set of four Eights got it, the other set of four would be upset, and there'd be fighting and tears."

"With Petal there's always tears no matter what's going on," Rebecca said.

We ignored Rebecca.

"Georgia, Jackie, and Marcia," Annie directed, "you bring your suitcases to the medium bedroom on the right side of the Petes' bedroom.

"Durinda, Petal, Rebecca, and Zinnia," Annie directed, "you bring your suitcases to the medium bedroom on the left side of the Petes' bedroom. Oh, and Rebecca, since you're the strongest, get mine too and put it in the right-hand bedroom."

"Why can't you carry your own suitcase?" Rebecca objected.

"Someone has to organize things so that everything goes smoothly, doesn't she?" Annie said. "Besides, I thought you enjoyed showing off your strength."

Annie consulted her unpacking manifest.

"Mrs. Pete," Annie directed, we must say in a lot more polite tone than the one she used to direct us, "could you get the bag with the beach items in it so we'll be ready to go just as soon we do a few other things here?"

"What do you mean by 'a few other things'?" Georgia said. "We're nearly done unpacking. Why can't we go as soon as we're done?"

Annie ignored Georgia, which gave us pause. What could Annie be referring to with her 'few other things'?

It was ominous. And while we'd grown accustomed to ominous things from evil persons and others outside our immediate circle of friends, we hated the idea of something ominous coming from a family member.

"Where do you want Daddy Sparky and Mommy Sally?" Pete asked, one under each arm. Apparently, while we were talking, Pete had anticipated the next item on Annie's unpacking manifest.

Annie tapped the end of her pen against her lower lip thoughtfully. We thought it showed her ability to think like an adult that she didn't tap with the nib of the pen, which would no doubt have resulted in blue lips.

"I think," Annie said at last, "that you should pose them in those two comfy chairs in front of the sliding glass doors. That way they can have a prime view of us when we play later on the beach — you know, after we finish doing a few other things."

What *other things?*

"It's not really possible to sit the suit of armor down in a chair," Pete called over, "but the dressmaker's dummy is very bendy." Pete brushed off his hands. "There, that's done," he said cheerily. "I think that's everything from the car."

"It can't be everything," Annie said, looking panicked as she consulted her unpacking manifest. "What about that box I asked you to pack?"

"Oh, right," Pete said, striking the heel of his palm against his forehead. We hoped he hadn't hurt himself. "How could I have forgotten that heavy box?"

As Pete went to fetch it, we wondered what it could

contain. Mentally, we ticked off items on our own un-packing manifests: bathing suits, flip-flops, towels, sun-glasses, hats, sunscreen, toothbrushes and toothpaste, shorts and T-shirts, one dress each in case a fancy occasion arose, pajamas, slippers, things with which to entertain ourselves. We already had everything we needed, we thought. So what could be in that box?

We didn't have to wonder much longer, because just then Pete returned, lugging the item in question.

"Where do you want it?" Pete asked Annie.

"Anywhere is fine," Annie said.

As soon as Pete set it down, Annie yanked open the top.

"There!" she said happily, pulling out a very large book—the size of a coloring book, only about five hundred pages long—and placing it beside her, giving it a happy pat as though greeting an old friend. Then she pulled out a second copy of the exact same book and handed it to Durinda.

Durinda turned pale when she saw what she had been given.

The same thing happened with Georgia, Jackie, Marcia, Rebecca, and Zinnia.

The same thing also happened with Petal, except Petal added the bloodcurdling shriek "Oh no! *Not Summer Workbook!*"

And then she fainted.

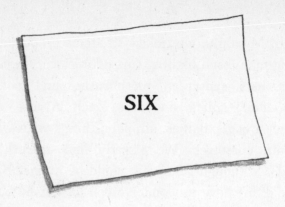

SIX

"Could someone please tell me what *Summer Workbook* is," Pete said, as Durinda and Jackie and Mrs. Pete fanned Petal back to consciousness, "and why its appearance here has managed to knock out Petal?"

"*Summer Workbook* is something our mother has us do," Marcia informed him.

"It's a workbook," Georgia said. "She has us do it every summer. That's why it's called *Summer Workbook*."

"She started this when we were very young," Zinnia said. "Sometimes I tell myself that *Summer Workbook* is like getting a present."

"Well, *I* don't tell myself that," Rebecca said. "In fact, I've told myself that the only good thing about this whole mess we've been in since New Year's Eve is that at least there won't be anyone around to make us do *Summer Workbook*." Rebecca made a disgusted face and added, "There's that dream out the window."

At all those repeated mentions of *Summer Workbook,* Petal fainted again.

More fanning on the parts of Durinda, Jackie, and Mrs. Pete. We hoped their arms weren't getting tired.

"I still don't understand," Pete said. Pete indicated the book next to Annie's side. "Can I see that, please?"

With reluctance, Annie handed it over.

"Summer Workbook." Pete read the title slowly, then he opened the cover and began paging through the book, reading out chapter headings along the way: "'Language Arts,' 'Spelling and Punctuation,' 'Reading Comprehension,' 'Vocabulary,' 'Mathematics,' 'Sample Tests.'" He flipped the book shut and studied the cover. "Hang on," he said. "It says here 'Grade Four.'" He looked up at us. "Isn't that the grade you're entering?"

"Yes," Annie said.

"I don't get it, then," Pete said. "Why would you spend the summer before fourth grade studying everything you're going to learn *in* fourth grade?"

"Don't you see?" Annie said. "That's the beauty of Mommy. Why do you think we're all so smart?" Annie cast a glance at Petal before adding, "Well, most of us. It's because each summer we go through the complete workbook for the grade we're about to enter. That's why we can keep up with our classmates so easily, even though they're all a year older than we are."

They're all—we had to silently chuckle at that. *All* constituted exactly two people, Will Simms and Mandy Stenko.

We sighed. We missed Will Simms. It would be nice to see him again before school started.

"Mommy always said," Jackie said, "that the smarter we became, the better our chances of taking over the world."

"And Daddy always said," Marcia added, "that it's important to have superior math skills so that if you get a modeling contract, you'll be able to know right away if someone is cheating you."

"Plus it's fun being smart," Annie said. "Both Mommy and Daddy said that."

"That all sounds like eminently sensible advice,"

Pete said, "but how long is this *Summer Workbook*? It looks like it's at least five hundred pages."

"It's actually five hundred and three," Annie said, "if you include the index."

"And you expect," Pete said, "yourself and your sisters to get through five hundred and three pages of *Summer Workbook* by the time you go back to school in — what — one month from now?"

"We go back to school on September second," Marcia corrected, "so actually it's a month from yesterday."

"I can't believe it's already August third," Zinnia said. "In just four weeks, it'll be August thirty-first. By then we should know what happened to Mommy and Daddy. Four weeks — it just seems both so long and so short away."

We ignored Zinnia.

"Normally," Annie said, "we'd have the whole summer to get the pages done. Mommy let us have the first week of summer vacation off, but then we'd do enough each day to get it done by September."

"Well," Pete said, "getting five hundred and three pages done in three months is a lot more reasonable than getting it done in one."

"I do know that," Annie said, looking guilty and then looking angry over being made to feel guilty. "But it's not really my fault. We were so busy in June and July, what with weddings and things getting set on fire and then needing to be put out, that I forgot all about it. But then, right when we decided to come to the Seaside, I remembered. That's why I went out to get the books."

At the mention of the word *Seaside,* seven Eights perked up.

We were at the Seaside . . . and the beach was right outside!

"Let's go swimming!" Zinnia said.

For once, we were all in agreement with Zinnia. Well, most of us were.

"We can't go *swimming* right now!" Annie was outraged. "We need to do *Summer Workbook*!"

"Not right this minute, we don't," Rebecca said, folding her arms across her chest. "I'm staging a revolt."

For once, we were all in agreement with Rebecca too.

"I revolt!" Durinda said.

"I revolt!" Georgia said.

"I revolt!" Jackie said.

"I revolt!" Marcia said.

"I revolt!" Petal said. Then she added, "Even though I'm not sure what that means."

"I revolt!" Zinnia said. "Let's go swimming!"

"But we have only thirty days to get through five hundred and three pages!" Annie said. "How many pages does that come to a day, Marcia? Quick, do the math."

"It comes to sixteen point seven six six, and on for as long as you can see sixes, pages," Marcia said. Then she saw fit to observe, "It would have been only five point five eight eight pages per day if you'd remembered to remind us to do *Summer Workbook* as soon as summer vacation began."

"Don't you see the urgency of the situation?" Annie said, appealing to Pete.

Apparently Annie thought she could drag an adult along for the ride in her madness. But Pete refused to be dragged.

"Sorry, pet," Pete said, "but I'm afraid I have to side with the revolters."

"But—" Annie started to protest, but Pete held up a hand, cutting her off. Some of us thought she was about to say that *revolters* wasn't a real word. It was, though. Some of us were very good with the vocabulary sections each summer.

"No buts," Pete said. "We came here to have a proper vacation, and a proper vacation we shall have. Now then." He clapped his hands. "All of you into your bathing suits."

Annie hung her head. Even Annie knew that you could appeal to an adult but you couldn't overrule one, not if the adult was Pete.

"Oh, don't look so glum, Annie," Pete said. "I promise, after we have a day of fun at the beach and a nice dinner and then perhaps some more fun, if you want to make your sisters do sixteen point seven six six and so on pages of *Summer Workbook* before retiring for the night, you just go for it."

LAST RESORT

SEVEN

We were all ready for the beach. We were standing on the deck and we had our bathing suits on, some of us in one-piece suits, some in bikinis. Well, Pete wasn't wearing a one-piece or a bikini. But he did have an inner tube in the shape of a sea serpent wrapped around his waist.

"I'm not much on swimming as such," Pete said when we looked pointedly at his serpent. "I prefer to just bob in the water."

We decided not to comment on the fact that Pete was wearing his work boots.

In addition to our bathing suits, we wore sunscreen, and we were carrying our towels. We also carried five beach umbrellas: Annie and Durinda had one, Georgia and Rebecca another, Jackie and Marcia a third, the Petes a fourth, and Zinnia struggled with one on her own, which was not easy to do with Call on one shoulder.

Poor Zinnia was struggling because one of us had yet to show up.

"Petal," Pete called into the house, "I'd hate to do anything to upset you, and I certainly wouldn't want to do anything to cause you to faint right now, but just what is taking you so long?"

We waited. And waited. And waited.

At last, at *long* last, Petal appeared.

Well, we assumed it was Petal inside and under all of that, but it was just an assumption.

"Petal?" Pete asked. "Is that you in there? And if so, what *are* you wearing?"

"I have on SPF one hundred plus zinc oxide on my nose," Petal said. "I have a floppy hat on my head, but I've also put sunscreen on the part in my hair and all around my ears, just in case. I am wearing a bathing suit from the early part of the nineteen hundreds, for modesty's sake; a towel wrapped around that; and a full-length terry-cloth robe over that. On my feet I have flip-flops, but I put my bunny slippers over those because the flip-flops don't give enough coverage. Oh, and I have on big dark sunglasses with the strongest UVF protection available."

"I have only one question," Pete said. "Why?"

"Because I don't want to burn, do I," Petal said. "You're not going to catch me exposing an inch of skin to the Seaside sun—not one inch! The Seaside sun, as everyone knows, is a very dangerous thing."

"You look like a mummy," Georgia said. "And your cat—poor Precious. Can Precious really breathe all wrapped up like that?"

"I knew it," Rebecca said. "I knew it!" She groaned. "This is going to be yet another of those vacations where everyone who sees us thinks we're all out of our tiny little minds, isn't it?"

* * * * * * * *

We settled ourselves on towels under our respective beach umbrellas, all except for Zinnia, who sat up and talked to Call.

Well, of course she did.

"Are there really eight Other Eights," Zinnia asked Call, "and where are they from?"

We had no idea why Zinnia would assume that Call knew a thing about the Other Eights. More crazy talk as far as we were concerned.

"Are they from Pittsburgh?" Zinnia persisted. "Vietnam? Spain? I'm almost certain they can't be from France. If they were, they'd have been at the wedding of Aunt Martha and Uncle George."

"Ask Call if they're from England, like Annie's faux-Daddy accent," Rebecca suggested.

"Ha! Ha!" Georgia said.

"You shouldn't mock Zinnia like that," Jackie said. "She can't help being the way she is. It's just too much for one person: all of the stress of being the only Eight to have to get her power and gift in the same month

· 66 ·

we all have our eighth birthday and after which we're supposed to discover how Mommy and Daddy disappeared."

"Or died," Rebecca put in.

"It's just too much stress for one Eight," Jackie stressed again, ignoring Rebecca. "No wonder Zinnia feels the need to acquire pigeon pets and pretend she can talk to those same pigeon pets."

"I heard that, Jackie," Zinnia said. Shockingly, her voice lacked a tone of offense as she added, "And it's not a pigeon pet. I keep telling you, it's a pigeon friend."

"I'm sorry," Jackie said.

"That's okay," Zinnia said.

"Why be sorry?" Georgia said. "And why is it okay? All any of this is is more crazy talk!"

"Has anyone else noticed," Jackie said, "that whenever we're all together, which is pretty much every minute of our waking lives, all we do is make fun of one another?"

"Oh, come on, Jackie," Durinda said. "We do support each other sometimes. It's not that bad."

Jackie thought about this for a moment.

"Yes," she finally said. "I really do think it is that bad." Then she grew excited. "I know!" she said. "I propose we spend a half an hour—no, a full hour—during which all we say is kind things about one another. Anyone else game?"

We didn't know if we were game, not exactly. But those waves in the ocean looked very choppy. So, sure. We were willing to play along.

"Okay," Jackie said excitedly, "who's ready to go first?"

Well, when she put it like *that* . . .

"Fine," Jackie said when it was clear no one was going to volunteer, "I'll go first. And I'll say that . . . let's see . . . that Georgia's naturally curly hair is most attractive on her. And further, when Georgia puts her mind to it, she can be quite sweet."

"Thanks, Jackie," Georgia said, "although it did sound as though you had to reach for that last part. Looks as though we're playing upward, meaning we're supposed to say something nice about the Eight in birth order ahead of us. That should be easy. Durinda makes a mean chocolate chip pancake. Phew, I'm glad that's over. It's not so easy being nice for an extended period of time."

"I may not always agree with Annie's tactics," Durinda contributed, "but I respect the fact that since New Year's Eve she's run this family pretty much as well as any adult could."

"Zinnia is sweet," Annie said, "probably the sweetest Eight we've got, but I do worry about this thinking-she-can-talk-to-cats-and-birds thing. That can't be healthy."

Zinnia was kind enough to ignore that last part, merely saying, "Rebecca is not nearly as nasty as she pretends to be."

Whenever one of us was called upon to say something nice about Rebecca, this not-nearly-as-nasty-as-she-pretends-to-be thing was pretty much all we could come up with. We didn't say it because we knew it was true; it was more because we hoped it might be.

"Great," Rebecca said. "That's just great. How am I supposed to follow that high praise?" She turned to Petal in her mummy costume. "I'm sorry!" Rebecca cried at last. "But I just can't do it! How can you expect me to say something positive about *that?*"

We looked where she was looking, at Petal. We kind of did understand what Rebecca meant.

"Fine," Petal said, rising to her feet as best she could in her mummy costume. "If no one can think of anything nice to say about me, I'll take myself off for a bit. I'll . . . I'll . . . I'll go for a walk."

And off Petal walked, as best she could.

"Well, that's just great," Jackie said, looking dejected as Petal trudged away in her bunny slippers through the sand. "We couldn't get through one whole round of the family being nice to one another without one of us saying something insulting, never mind lasting a whole hour. How long did we last, a whole five minutes?"

"Maybe it was six," Zinnia said optimistically.

"Actually, I'm fairly certain it was five minutes and twenty-seven seconds," Marcia said, apparently consulting some internal clock that was extremely precise. Then she frowned. "Or was that twenty-eight seconds?"

"We're sorry, Jackie," Durinda said. "And here, no one even got the chance to say anything nice about you."

"Or me," Marcia added.

"I don't care," Jackie said, and we could tell she didn't. Jackie was just like that. "But look at Petal."

We looked. There went Petal, trudging farther and farther away from us in her bunny slippers. Why, she was so far away, she practically looked like a normal person.

"Back home," Jackie went on, "Petal sometimes asks for an escort just to go to the bathroom—and it's our bathroom in our house! And now here she is going off by herself without any family protection. Where *can* she be going?"

* * * * * * * *

A half-hour later, or what seemed like a half-hour, Petal trudged back, breathless.

"Petal," Jackie said, "what's wrong?"

"Someone was following me," Petal said, still trying to catch her breath.

"Following you?" seven Eights plus the Petes cried in concern. "But who? Why?"

"If I knew that," Petal said, "I would tell you. All I know is, every time I took a step, the shadow behind me took a step too." Petal paused and then burst out with "I have a stalker!"

Oh, Petal.

"Oh, Petal," even Jackie felt forced to say. "Of course you don't have a stalker. You must be seeing your own shadow. Why, look how low the sun is in the sky."

Petal looked, stopped, wondered.

"There's the positive thing I have to say about Petal," Rebecca said. "Petal's so scared of everything, she's scared of her own shadow. I don't know about the rest of you, but I think it's kind of *cute!*"

And so ended the first full day of our vacation, August 3. Well, we did have a bonfire on the beach, over which we cooked fish dogs and toasted marshmallows — Pete found a Seaside store where he could do a Big Shop — and Petal worried that the bonfire would kill us all, and then we went back to our rooms and did 16.766 pages of various parts of the workbook, just to please Annie and because we liked to skip around in *Summer Workbook,* and then we went to sleep.

But really, we would think later, the day might just as well have ended when Rebecca insulted Petal by assuming that Petal was merely scared of her own shadow.

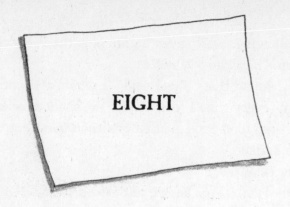

EIGHT

It was the next morning, August 4.

"I'm hungry!" Annie announced.

"I'm hungry!" Georgia announced.

"I'm hungry!" Jackie announced.

"I'm hungry!" Marcia announced.

"I'm hungry!" Petal announced.

"I'm hungry!" Rebecca announced.

"I'm hungry!" Zinnia announced.

"I must say," Pete said, patting his belly, "I'm a bit hungry myself."

"It's odd," Mrs. Pete added, "but fish dogs don't stick with a person as long as a person might think they would."

"Well, don't look at me," Durinda said. "I'm not going to make everyone's breakfast. It's supposed to be my vacation too, after all."

We all turned to Jackie, sure she'd bail us out. And we were sure she was about to, since she was smiling and had opened her mouth to speak. But before any words could come out, someone else spoke.

"Fine," Georgia said. "I'll make breakfast for everybody."

We gaped at her. *Georgia— Georgia,* who never did anything resembling a chore unless sternly commanded to by Annie—was offering to make us all breakfast?

Our gaping continued as Georgia headed into the kitchen, and our gaping continued yet further at the ensuing racket that came from that room. The sound of cabinets opening and slamming shut, drawers being yanked out and slid in, the clatter of crockery, and the tinkling of silverware.

"She must be making us a feast in there," Annie said in a hushed voice.

"What's that other sound?" Jackie asked.

"Is Georgia humming?" Petal asked.

"No," Marcia corrected. "She's whistling. Georgia's whistling while she's working."

"Huh," Durinda said, sounding miffed. "I never whistle while I work."

"Is everyone ready for breakfast?" Georgia shouted to us.

We don't feel the need to recount our individual responses here. Suffice to say that basically we all shouted back, "Yes!"

"Ready or not," Georgia called, "here comes breakfast!"

A moment later Georgia emerged from the kitchen bearing a tray upon which sat two bowls, two spoons, a box, and ten juice boxes. She handed the bowls, which we now saw contained cereal, to the Petes and the box to Annie.

"Sorry," Georgia said, "but the little cottage doesn't come with service for ten, so I figured it was only fair that the Petes get the two bowls, since they are old."

"Old*er*," Annie corrected with a smile toward the Petes, as though to prove the rest of us weren't as bad as, well, Georgia. "Georgia just means you're older than us and therefore worthy of respect."

Good save, Annie!

"What's this feast you've prepared for us?" Rebecca demanded of Georgia as we each reached for a juice box, pleased to see it was mango.

"Razzle Crunchies, of course," Georgia said, "the official cereal of the Sisters Eight."

"You made all that noise in the kitchen," Durinda said, "just to wind up serving us a box of Razzle Crunchies?"

"It was a very involved process," Georgia said. "Anyway, I thought it was rather wonderful that Mr. Pete was able to find Razzle Crunchies at the little Seaside grocery store. I always assumed Razzle Crunchies were a delicacy available for sale only in the town where we live. Now, eat up, everybody, so we can get to the beach."

"But how are we supposed to eat up," Rebecca said, "when the Petes are the only ones with bowls and Annie's holding the box?"

"Oh, right," Georgia said. "Well, since there are only two bowls, we're supposed to just pass the box among ourselves and shove our hands in and grab what we like." Georgia turned to Annie. "Do you think you could stop hogging the box now?"

"Sor*ry,*" Annie said, grabbing a handful and handing the box to Durinda, who accepted the box grudgingly.

"When *I* make breakfast," Durinda muttered, "it doesn't go like this."

"Um, terrific breakfast, Georgia," Pete said politely around a mouthful of Razzle and Crunch.

"Where's Call?" Zinnia said suddenly, looking worried. "I haven't seen him since last night. Call! Call!"

"Oh no," Petal said. "Call is probably one of those traitor pigeon pets you're always hearing about in the news. Probably right this minute Call is off somewhere trading our secrets with the enemy in exchange for better pigeon food."

We ignored Petal.

"Call! Call!" Zinnia shouted as she moved from room to room.

We wished we could ignore Zinnia too, and we would have if she hadn't been shouting so loudly.

"Call! Ca—"

"Oh, good," Jackie said. "Zinnia must have found Call, because she's stopped shouting."

"Or else she found Call dead," Rebecca added, then added some more. "Or else Zinnia's dead."

But as it turned out, neither dire outcome was the case, which we saw when Zinnia entered with Call perched on her shoulder.

"Where did you find Call?" Jackie asked.

"Outside," Zinnia said happily, "with the cats. Call and Zither were having a conversation. I think they were trying to get to know each other better."

Oh, Zinnia.

* * * * * * * *

"Isn't anyone going in the water?" Pete asked.

We were back on the beach again, in the same spot we'd been in the day before. We all had our bathing suits on, except for Petal, who had on — well, you know.

"I said," Pete said, "isn't anyone going in the water? No one went in yesterday."

We ignored Pete, although what he said was true. We hadn't gone in yesterday, and we weren't going in today, because, well, we were somewhat scared of the water here. Back home, we didn't have an ocean. Back home, all we had was a wading pool we'd outgrown and that had never been scary in the first place, except maybe to Petal. But this, this . . . *ocean* — it was so vast. We couldn't even see where it ended. We were scared of things we couldn't see the end of, the great uncertainty of it all.

"This is so odd," Pete said. "Why come to the Seaside and then just sit by the side part and not go in the sea part?"

"But there are plenty of other things to do by the side of the sea," Annie pointed out.

"Things that are even more fun than actually going into the sea," Durinda added.

"Like what?" Pete said.

"We could play beach volleyball," Jackie suggested.

"I'm fairly certain that's something people do at the side of the sea," Marcia added.

"Do you see a volleyball or a net anywhere?" Georgia scoffed.

We didn't mind so much her scoffing at Marcia, but we rather did mind her scoffing at Jackie.

"Why don't we bury Petal up to her neck in the sand?" Rebecca suggested. "Burying people up to their necks in the sand is definitely a by-the-sea activity, and anyway, with all the clothes Petal's wearing, she's practically buried already."

"Oh no," Petal said forcefully. "You won't catch me letting myself be buried in the sand. That's a terribly dangerous thing for a person to allow to happen to herself. A passing pigeon might think my head was a perch, and then where would I be? I'd be known as Petal the Pigeon Perch. It would be so embarrassing."

We didn't think anything could be more embarrassing than the outfit Petal was wearing.

"Or else," Petal went on, "you might bury me and then all decide you wanted to get snow cones. So you'd run off to do that, leaving me here alone, and then you wouldn't be able to find me again later because all I'd be is a tiny head in the crowd and I'd be stuck here the rest of my life."

We hadn't thought the fear of being a pigeon perch could be topped, but somehow she'd managed to do it.

"Or else—" Petal started in on yet another new fear, but Rebecca cut her off.

"Fine," Rebecca said. "You can all bury me, then. I don't mind. *I* think it would be rather fun to be buried."

So that's what we did, buried Rebecca up to her neck in the sand. We had to admit: burying Rebecca was rather fun. In fact, we wondered why we hadn't thought of it earlier.

"Now what?" Georgia asked, once Rebecca was entirely covered up to her neck, only her head remaining visible. "Do we just sit around here and stare at your head all day, Rebecca? The burying part was fun but I don't see staring at your head all day as being much of a game."

"I think," Zinnia said, slowly rising to her feet, "I'll take a little dip in the ocean."

What?

"What?" Pete said.

We hadn't told Pete about our fear—of course we hadn't told him that—but the tone of his voice told us he'd picked up on it on his own. It was funny how Pete could be intelligent like that at times.

"It'll just be a little dip," Zinnia said, heading toward the water's edge. "I shouldn't be too long."

"Don't go too far!" Pete shouted after her. "Do you

see those buoys bobbing a little ways out? Don't go past that line!"

Without turning, Zinnia waved her hand in the air, acknowledging that she'd heard Pete.

We watched with interest as Zinnia stood at the edge of the water and got her toes wet. We watched with interest as she kicked at the water playfully with her feet. We watched with interest as she began walking out into the water, jumping over tiny waves as they came at her.

"Don't go too far out!" Pete shouted again, rising to his feet as Zinnia waded farther into the ocean.

We'd been doing a lot of watching with interest, but now we watched in horror as a dark shape beneath the surface of the water made straight for Zinnia.

"Oh no!" Petal shouted. "It's a shark!"

"Shark!" Pete shouted, running toward the water. "Zinnia, get out of the water!"

"Shark!" we all shouted, including Mrs. Pete, as we all ran after Pete.

"Shark!" Rebecca's head shouted.

We'd never run so fast in our lives, and as we ran, we saw more dark shapes beneath the surface heading straight for Zinnia. But why wasn't Zinnia moving? Why wasn't she running from the ocean? Why wasn't she trying to save herself?

And then, as we plunged into the surf, heedless of the danger to ourselves in our quest to save Zinnia, we saw that the dark shapes weren't sharks at all.

We froze where we were, stared.

Under a sky so perfectly blue it might have been colored with one of the crayons from our box back home, and as the sunlight shimmered on the ocean, making sparkling diamond spots on the green waves, we saw that what we'd thought were sharks were dolphins, all swimming around Zinnia as though she were one of them.

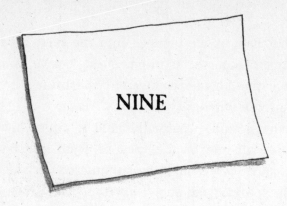

NINE

Pete let out a low whistle.

"I'd never believe this," Pete said, "if I weren't seeing it with my own eyes."

We'd heard Pete say similar things on a few previous occasions, whenever he witnessed the results of one of us getting her power.

Well, we knew this couldn't be that. This was simply . . . whatever it was.

"Dolphins don't typically come in this close to the shore," Pete said.

"I wouldn't have thought they could," Mrs. Pete said.

We ignored the Petes, overcoming our frozen state to join Zinnia amid the dolphins.

"What about me?" Rebecca's head shouted to us.

We ignored Rebecca's head too.

We'd heard the word *frolic* before, but we couldn't say it was an activity any of us had ever engaged in. We did so now, however, frolicking in the ocean with

Zinnia and the dolphins and even the Petes, who were frolicking too.

The dolphins were so beautiful, with their gray skin and their wide mouths that looked like great big smiles. And they were so friendly too. They did seem to like Zinnia better than they liked the rest of us put together, but they didn't entirely ignore us. In fact, they let us pet them, and they didn't spit on us, so we figured they must like us well enough.

"What about me?" Rebecca's head shouted.

"These may not be sharks," Petal said, suddenly sounding worried, "but what's that black thing heading toward us?"

We looked up in time to see the dark fin snaking its way to us.

Now we froze in fear.

All except for Zinnia, that is, who tilted her head to one side, frowning at the approaching fin.

The fin abruptly ceased approaching, turned, and headed out to sea again.

"How odd," Annie said as we all relaxed.

"How lucky," Durinda said.

Zinnia said nothing.

"This is so much fun," Jackie said, petting a dolphin.

"Almost as much fun as getting caught in an avalanche," Georgia admitted.

"I wonder how many dolphins there are here," Marcia said. "Maybe I should count them?"

"I would like to stay and keep doing this," Petal said, "but the water has waterlogged my bathrobe and all the other clothes I've got on, and I do believe I'm about to slip beneath the surface and drown."

It was a testament to how peaceful it was being surrounded by dolphins who were so gentle they were willing to frolic with us that Petal said this in such an even tone of voice. Why, she hardly sounded scared at all. Perhaps she was just joking.

But when we turned to look at her, we could see she was barely keeping her head above the water.

"Petal!" Annie cried. Then she turned to us. "Quick, we have to get Petal out of here!"

Five of us plus the Petes clasped our arms together under Petal to create a stretcher upon which to carry her out.

"It looks like you've got that under control," Zinnia said from her place among the dolphins. "Does anyone mind if I just stay out here for a few more minutes?"

* * * * * * * *

A few more minutes later, Zinnia was still in the water while the rest of us had finished dragging the sodden

Petal back and had placed her on a spot under our beach umbrellas.

Well, all of us except for one, and by *one* we don't mean Zinnia . . .

"How inconsiderate!" Rebecca's head snapped at us. "You all went off to . . . *frolic,* and you left me here by myself in the sand. You could have dug me out first."

"You know you could have used your own super-human strength to dig yourself out of the sand," Georgia countered.

"Huh," Rebecca said. "I hadn't even thought of that."

"Besides," Jackie said, "it's not like it would have been nice for us to stop to dig you out when we thought Zinnia was about to get eaten by a shark."

"What does *nice* have to do with anything?" Rebecca said.

"What's this?" Marcia said.

"What's what?" Rebecca said.

"Behind your head," Marcia said. "There's what looks suspiciously like a note here."

"Well, how could I have seen it if it's *behind* my head?" Rebecca said.

"But didn't you hear anyone come up behind you and leave it there?" Annie said.

We saw the sand around Rebecca ripple and realized she'd just shrugged, exercising her superhuman strength against the weight of the sand. In fact, she'd shrugged so hard, she'd shrugged her shoulders free, and soon she pulled her arms out as well.

"I was too busy watching you all—first running and then freezing and then frolicking and then freezing again and so forth—to notice what was going on behind me," Rebecca said.

"Oh no!" Marcia cried, ignoring Rebecca.

Huh, we thought. "Oh no!" was usually Petal's line.

"Oh no!" Marcia cried again, and now we could see that she'd opened the note and was reading it. She read it to us:

Dear Zinnia,

Still enjoying your power, I see — good show!

"The note leaver is still acting all kerflooey," Marcia said. "We all know that this isn't Zinnia's power, that this thing with the dolphins is just—I don't know— *something else,* but the note leaver keeps acting like it *is* her power."

We looked from the note to Zinnia frolicking with the dolphins. We knew Marcia was right. Zinnia couldn't communicate with animals. They just liked her. That's all it was.

"Oh, we can't let Zinnia see this," Marcia said.

"But it was addressed to her," Annie said.

"I agree with Marcia," Rebecca said, pulling herself all the way out of the sand. "Zinnia's always been the nuttiest Eight." Rebecca paused to look at Petal, who was on all fours shaking back and forth in her bathrobe like a dog trying to rid itself of water, which she had plenty of right now. "Well, one of the two nuttiest Eights," Rebecca corrected herself. "Always believing she could talk to the cats, then thinking she could talk to that stupid pigeon pet, and now this thing with the dolphins. On top of that, there're these notes that keep coming, talking about her power. If she sees this latest one, right after that thing with the dolphins, we'll never be able to convince her that she *can't* communicate with animals. And if she goes on believing she *can* communicate with animals, eventually she'll be labeled crazy, we'll have to lock her away in a lunatic asylum, and there goes the whole family reputation."

"I think that ship has sailed," Jackie said, "on more than one voyage."

"My, that was a long speech," Georgia said to Rebecca.

"Yes, well," Rebecca said, "a person has a long time to think when she's buried up to her head in sand all alone while everyone else is playing."

"But you didn't know about the note at that time,"

Georgia said, "so how could you have been thinking this out then?"

"I wasn't," Rebecca said. She shrugged. "I guess it's just the leftover effects from before of having more time on my hands to think. My brain must still be doing that."

"Never mind all that right now," Marcia said, exasperated. "Who cares what Rebecca's brain is doing? The important thing is to get this note away from here before Zinnia comes back and sees it."

"You'd better hurry, then," Georgia said, looking toward the ocean, "because she's coming out now."

We looked up in time to see Zinnia wave to the dolphins before turning in our direction.

"Oh," Petal said, sounding exasperated as she struggled to her feet, "I'll take it."

"*You'll* take it?"

Okay, we all said that, including the Petes. We were that shocked: Petal offering to go off by herself again, Petal volunteering for a mission.

"What's wrong with that?" Petal said. "I did manage to walk by myself yesterday without disaster striking. Well, there was that little problem with the shadow, but since you did all convince me it was just my own . . ." Petal held her hand out for Marcia to give her the note. "Besides," Petal added, shaking her arms, "the walk will do me good. Maybe I'll finally be able to lose the rest of this water weight."

* * * * * * * *

"What have you all been up to?" Zinnia asked, joining us a moment later.

The words Zinnia spoke were innocent enough in and of themselves, and even the way she delivered them sounded perfectly normal.

Still, we couldn't escape the sense of guilt washing over us as we kicked the sand with our feet, hands clasped behind our backs.

"Nothing much," we said, hoping we sounded innocent too.

* * * * * * * *

Petal didn't sound at all innocent when she returned to us. She sounded frightened. And angry.

"You were all wrong," she said. "There was somebody following me yesterday. I know that because the same person followed me today."

Oh, Petal.

"It's true," she insisted, reading our Oh-Petal expressions accurately. "I went a ways down the beach to bury"—she paused, cast a look at Zinnia—"you know, something unimportant in the sand. Walking there I didn't notice anything funny, probably because my mind was occupied by my mission." She cast another glance at Zinnia, adding, "My thoroughly unimportant mission. But on my way back, when my mind was no longer occupied, I saw the shadow again."

"We already explained to you yesterday," Annie pointed out with a surprising degree of patience, "that's your own shadow."

"No, it's not," Petal said. "I took my own shadow into account, and this shadow wasn't my shadow. Every time I'd take a step, my shadow and this other shadow would take a step too. Every time I stopped taking steps, my shadow and this other shadow would also stop. Whenever I tried to turn around, though, to catch the person in the act, I couldn't see anybody behind me. Whoever this shadow person is, he or she must be very fast and good at hiding. Anyway, my shadow and this other shadow followed me all the way here."

We all craned our necks to peer around Petal.

"Well," Pete said gently, "if another shadow followed you all the way here, it must have escaped fairly quickly and been invisible in the first place, because you're the only one standing in front of us and there's no second shadow behind you."

"Perhaps," Mrs. Pete suggested, just as gently, "you've spent too much time overdressed in the sun, dear?"

"I know what I saw," Petal said, turning in circles to try to catch this imaginary other shadow, "even if none of you see it now and I don't either. What if it's someone dangerous that's following me in the hopes of worming secrets out of me? What if it's Bill Collector or, worse, what if it's finally the ax murderer? What if—"

"We'll all go for a walk with you this time," Annie suggested. "We'll walk with you and we'll keep count of all our shadows as we walk. If someone is following you—or us—we'll catch that person."

We expected Rebecca to say something snide about Annie humoring the loony, but she didn't. We figured that for once Rebecca had seen the wisdom of Annie's ways and recognized the fact that Annie was right: if we didn't do something to humor the loony, and fast, Petal would never stop going on about this.

* * * * * * * *

So we walked.

We walked, and walked, and walked.

"We have ten shadows," Annie had announced heartily when we first started walking. But as the day went on, and the walking continued, the heartiness of those

·91·

announcements waned to something less enthusiastic, like "Yup, still just ten shadows."

"Can we stop for a snack?" Georgia said.

"Is it tomorrow yet?" Rebecca said. "Perhaps this is all just one big nightmare I'm having."

"I don't like to complain," Zinnia said, "but my feet are getting a bit tired."

"Maybe—" Jackie started to say.

We never did learn what sensible Jackie had to contribute because just then Petal said in an urgent whisper, "There it is! There's the shadow!"

We stopped walking and began counting shadows. We counted again.

Petal was right: there *was* an eleventh shadow!

"It's the same shadow I saw yesterday and today," Petal whispered, still urgently. "And as you can see, it's nothing like my shadow."

It was true. This eleventh shadow had nowhere near the bulk of Petal's bathrobe shadow.

Ten heads swiveled around abruptly. We admit it, we half expected to see no one there, just as Petal said happened every time she tried to catch the person following her. We half expected to learn there was nothing following us but a mysterious shadow, which would have been scary in its own way.

How funny, then, to turn around and see . . .

"A *boy?*" Annie said.

There was a boy behind us, and no one else in sight. Or at least not in sight behind us. The boy had on a bathing suit and sandals. He had brown hair and brown eyes, kind of like us. If we had to say how tall he was, we'd have said he was closest to Georgia in height. In fact, his hair was most similar to Georgia's as well.

The boy was smiling at us.

"Who are you?" Annie demanded.

"George," the boy said, still smiling.

That seemed odd. *George . . . Georgia . . .*

"Have you been following Petal?" Annie said, still using her demanding voice.

"I might have been," the boy named George said, still smiling, "but not for anything bad." Abruptly, he raised his hand, waved. "See you around!"

And then he turned and raced away from us down the beach, his body becoming smaller and smaller until it was finally invisible as the orange sun disappeared from the sky.

"Huh," Annie said, hands on hips. "What do you think that was all about?"

"Maybe he has a crush on Petal," Durinda suggested.

Rebecca looked at Petal, snorted. "You cannot be serious."

We couldn't help it. We laughed too. The idea of that boy, the ridiculous idea of any boy, having a crush on Petal when she was wearing her Petal beach getup . . .

It took us a moment to realize one of us wasn't laughing, and by *one of us* we don't mean Petal, who apparently found this as uproarious as the rest of us.

"Whatever that boy George wanted," Zinnia said thoughtfully, "I don't think that was it."

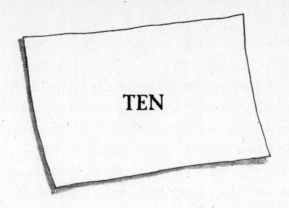

TEN

"No more excuses!" Annie shouted.

"Of course we can come up with more excuses," Rebecca countered. "Just give us time."

It was the following morning, August 5, and we'd finished breakfast and changed into our beach clothes because we were going to the beach right after breakfast.

Or so we thought.

Turned out, Annie had other plans for us.

And those other plans went by the seemingly innocent two-word phrase *Summer Workbook*.

"I don't care what other excuses you might be able to come up with," Annie said now, "because it doesn't matter. Yesterday we were so busy, what with frolicking with dolphins and trying to identify shadows, we never got around to getting our daily quota in. That means we're a full day behind schedule. That means a double dose today if we want to get it all done before school starts."

"But we don't want to get it done," Rebecca said.

"None of us do," Georgia added. "Well, except for you."

"It doesn't matter what you want or don't want," Annie said. "I'm in charge and I say we need to do double. Now then, two times sixteen point seven six six comes to how much?" Annie looked to Marcia.

"Don't tell her!" six Eights shouted at Marcia.

But we needn't have bothered.

"Thirty-three point five three two," Marcia answered promptly. Then she turned to us with an apologetic shrug. "Sorry," she said. "I just can't help myself."

Annie ignored the last part of what Marcia said, responding only to the part that mattered to her.

"That's right," Annie said. "So if we're going to get thirty-three point five three two pages done today, we really do need to—"

"Excuse me," Jackie said, cutting Annie off, which was a brave thing to do. Almost no one cut off Annie. "I don't mean to offend you, Annie, but we've all been wondering: Why are you the way you are?"

It was true. We had been wondering. Not only had we been wondering, but just that morning we'd been discussing it among ourselves while Annie was in the bathroom. At the end of the discussion, we'd nominated Jackie to talk to Annie about it. Okay, we begged Jackie to, because the rest of us were too scared to take Annie on about anything in general and this in particular.

"Excuse me?" Annie said now, sternly.

"It's just that," Jackie said gently, "we do remember what you were like before Mommy and Daddy disappeared. True, you've always been the oldest. And, being the oldest, you did tend to be bossy when compared to, say, Petal. But not like this. Not this constant need to be in charge of every little thing. Not this constant need to control everything we do and make sure everyone does your bidding. I hate to say it, but at times it makes it difficult to like you. We always love you, but this morning you are making liking you very hard. We just want to have a good vacation. Don't you want to have a good vacation too?"

As Jackie spoke, we watched Annie's face change from stern to confused and finally to sad. Even the least observant of us marked these changes. And then that made us sad, not just for Annie but also for Jackie, who we knew never liked to be the cause of sadness in anyone else.

Oh no. Was that a tear in Annie's eye?

"Do you have any idea," Annie said, her voice quavering, "how hard these past seven months and five days have been on me? I knew *someone* had to take charge of leading the family in Mommy's and Daddy's absence, or we'd all get split up. We'd lose each other. I did it because I felt I had to, so our lives wouldn't turn to chaos and ruin. But do you honestly think I enjoy being thought of as the bossy Eight?"

"Yes," Rebecca said, "I do think that."

"That's not helpful," Jackie told Rebecca as she put her arm around Annie.

"You're right," Rebecca said. "I don't honestly think she enjoys being thought of as the bossy Eight. But I do think she enjoys being bossy. A lot."

"That's not helpful either," Jackie said.

"No, no," Annie said, sounding so very sad. "Rebecca's right. Perhaps I have enjoyed it too much, you know, being bossy."

Oh, we hated seeing Annie like this. Seeing Annie looking sad and broken was far worse than having her order us around. We were almost certain that, despite the nasty things she said, even Rebecca felt this way.

After Annie's tears and all that she'd said, we felt we understood her a little better. True, there was some choice in her behavior toward us, but mostly it just had to do with her being her. Why, Annie couldn't stop herself from acting as though she were in charge of everything any more than Marcia could stop herself from blurting out the answer to 2 times 16.766. It was just her nature.

Suddenly, we felt we *had* to do something to make Annie feel good.

"You know, Annie," Zinnia said, "I really do feel like doing *Summer Workbook*."

"If you dry your tears," Petal promised, "I'll get out my *Summer Workbook* right now."

"I know we only just had breakfast a short time ago," Durinda offered, "but I could make us all a snack for extra brainpower while we work."

"I'll go get the pencils," Georgia offered.

"This is great," Marcia said when we all had our pencils and workbooks in front of us. "I *love* doing *Summer Workbook*!"

"There's no need to lay it on quite that thick, Marcia," Rebecca said.

"What are you talking about?" Marcia said. "I *do* love doing *Summer Workbook*." Marcia gave a happy sigh. "I just love learning things."

"Could someone look at my forehead?" Petal said. "I feel as though my brain is expanding already and I am worried it might be beginning to bulge."

Oh, Petal.

Jackie studied the proffered forehead kindly. "No worries," Jackie said. "It looks like your brain is probably still the same size."

Annie cleared her throat. "You do know," she said,

"that I do love all of you and that's partly why I am the way I am, right?"

Yeah. We did know that.

Just then there came a rumble of thunder followed by a downpour of rain, sheets of it.

"That roof never did look sound," Pete said. "I'll go find some buckets to catch the water that's leaking through the ceiling."

While Pete did that, Petal grabbed one of Pete's work boots and placed it under the biggest leak. "Stinky but effective," she pronounced.

It was a good thing, we thought as lightning crackled through the sky, that we hadn't left for the beach.

And it was a good thing, we thought as it continued to rain throughout the day, that we had something with which to keep ourselves occupied inside.

* * * * * * * *

It is funny how summer can affect a person's brain. You go through the school year, learning all sorts of things, and then summer comes and you think: *Well, that's enough of that for now. Yippee!*

But doing *Summer Workbook* that day as a summer storm raged outside reminded us of all we'd been missing, the excitement of learning about new things a person hadn't even dreamed existed.

By the time Zinnia lifted her head up, we'd long passed the combined quota for that day and the day before, and none of us had complained about all the work we were doing, not once, not even Rebecca. Perhaps we hadn't complained because we were too busy having fun seeing how much we did know and how much we could know.

"What's this?" Zinnia asked, her finger marking a spot on the page.

We all gathered round Zinnia and saw that she was working in the Mathematics section.

"It's an infinity symbol," Annie said.

"Yes, I know that," Zinnia said. "I can read the caption under the diagram as well as you can, but I still don't understand what it means or what it does."

"Sorry, I haven't gotten to that page in Mathematics yet," Annie said. "I've been working mostly in other sections. Marcia?"

But it turned out Marcia hadn't gotten to that page in Mathematics yet because she'd been too busy focusing on getting through Language Arts all in one go. None of the rest of us had gotten to that page either.

So we did the sensible thing.

We read what the page had to say about infinity, some of us reading more quickly than others. We waited for those others to finish.

"If I understand correctly," Jackie said, "*infinity* is a word meaning an unlimited extent of time, space, or

quantity. So that symbol in relation to numbers is like saying that the number in question is endless. If you could
live forever and count forever during that forever life, the
number would still be going on."

"Huh," Zinnia said. "It's still a bit confusing, but somewhat less so than before."

Zinnia tilted her head to one side, studying the symbol
on the page from a new angle. "Huh," she said again.
"When you look at it this way, the infinity symbol looks a
bit like an eight lying down."

Seven more heads tilted, plus the heads of the Petes,
who'd come in just then to check on us.

We saw that Zinnia was right. An infinity symbol did
look like an eight lying down.

"I wonder," Zinnia said, "if we could make our own
infinity symbol."

"Could you show us what you have in mind, Zinnia?"
Annie said somewhat formally.

How odd for Annie to speak to one of us like that, we
thought. And then we realized what Annie was doing: she
was trying to let one of us be in charge of something for
a change.

"Let's clear a big space in the middle of the floor," Zinnia suggested.

We did that.

"Now let's arrange ourselves," Zinnia said, "like we're
one big eight."

"Do you want us to be an infinity symbol or one big eight?" Jackie asked.

Zinnia shrugged. "Both," she said.

"I'm not seeing this," Rebecca said.

We ignored Rebecca although we couldn't see it yet either.

"Annie," Zinnia directed, "lie down on your side and curve your body a little to form one curved end of the eight. Durinda, you hold on to Annie's ankles and curve your hands just slightly. Georgia, you hold on to Durinda's ankles so you can be the line in the center. Jackie, you hold on to Georgia's ankles to continue the line, but curve your legs a bit. Marcia, you grab on to Jackie's curved legs and curve your whole body like Annie's doing to form the other curved end of the eight. Petal, you grab on to Marcia's curved ankles and curve your hands slightly. Rebecca, you hold on to Petal's ankles so you can be the other line in the center, crossing Georgia's line. And now I'll hold on to Rebecca's ankles, and then Annie can grab on to mine when I curve them slightly, like so. There!"

Well, now that we were all in position . . .

"Do you see now?" Zinnia asked excitedly.

"How can I see anything," Rebecca said, "other than Petal's stinky feet. Petal, did you wash these today?"

"Well . . ." Petal said.

The Petes came over and studied the shape we were in on the floor.

"You know," Pete said after a long moment, "I can see it. The eight of you have joined together to form a single eight."

"But if I look at you this way," Mrs. Pete said, tilting her head, "you look like an eight lying down, or an infinity symbol."

"*That's* what I was getting at!" Zinnia said triumphantly.

"Since a few people finally get it," Georgia said, "can we stop doing this now?"

Not waiting for Zinnia's answer, we pulled apart from one another.

"I'm not being critical," Annie said, "but I am curious, Zinnia: what was that about?"

"I don't know." Zinnia shrugged. "Impulse?" she asked as much as answered. "I just suddenly felt as though we should do it, see if we *could* do it. In our world, you never know what might come in handy one day."

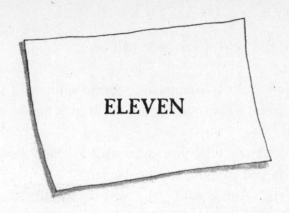

ELEVEN

Being able to turn our eight bodies into one infinity symbol may have felt like a potentially handy thing to know on August 5, but nothing could save us the next day, not when we woke up and realized . . .

It was August 6! Our eighth birthday was just *two days away,* and none of us had done a bit of shopping yet!

"Oh no!" Annie said, being the one to say "Oh no!" for once. Then she proceeded to explain the situation to the Petes.

"With our parents being . . . not around," she concluded after a fair bit of talking, "we'll have no presents for our birthday in two days."

"Of course you'll have presents, pet," Pete said gently.

"We will?" Annie said, shocked.

"Of course you will," Mrs. Pete said. "We have presents for you."

Oh, the Petes were good people.

But . . .

"That truly is wonderful," Annie said, "and we are not ungrateful, but we usually get things for each other as well."

"I don't see why you can't still do that," Pete said. "How do you propose we go about it?"

"Well," Annie said, "the way it usually works is Durinda, Georgia, Jackie, Marcia, Petal, Rebecca, and I go shopping for Zinnia. We go with Mommy while Zinnia stays home with Daddy. Then when we're done with that, Georgia, Jackie, Marcia—"

"I think I see the pattern already," Pete said. "What you're saying is that you go on eight separate shopping trips to get eight separate presents for each other, seven of you going off with your mother while that particular present recipient stays at home with your father."

We were grateful for Pete's quick grasp of the situation, for his immediate understanding of how we did things in our family. If he hadn't understood so fast, we would have waited while Annie listed the eight different casts of characters for the eight separate shopping trips.

We were also grateful, for once, for Annie's ability to take charge of a situation and explain what was required.

"Sure, we can do that," Pete said. "The seven shoppers on each trip will go with Mrs. Pete while I stay here with the particular present recipient."

We did find it odd that he referred to his own wife as Mrs. Pete, but in the face of his generosity we let it go.

"It does sound," Pete added, "as though such an involved shopping process could take all day."

* * * * * * * *

As it turned out, Pete was right.

It *did* take all day, going on eight separate shopping excursions, selecting the perfect present for each particular present recipient, and then getting each present wrapped before returning with it to the cottage.

In fact, we missed the whole day at the beach.

But it was worth it to ensure that at least one part of our birthday would be the same as it always had been in our family.

* * * * * * * *

We awoke the next morning, August 7, to a gorgeous summer day, the kind of day that would be perfect to spend at the beach. But we also awoke to . . .

"Why so glum, chums?" Pete asked.

It was true. We were glum again, depressed.

"I thought," Zinnia said, speaking for all of us, "that it

would be best to be away from home for our eighth birthday — you know, because Mommy and Daddy aren't with us this year. But I'm finding that as tomorrow looms closer, the idea of being away from home on our birthday is even worse, like it's just one change too many in our lives."

"Are you saying you want to go back early?" Pete asked.

"Yes, please," Zinnia said.

We gave her credit for having stellar manners in trying times.

"But we have this cottage for two more days," Mrs. Pete said gently.

"Even still," Zinnia said, "we would like to go today, if you don't mind."

"Of course we don't mind," Pete said.

"Of course we don't," Mrs. Pete said. "We only ever wanted to make you happy."

"So we'll just load up the car," Pete said.

"We won't forget Daddy Sparky and Mommy Sally," Mrs. Pete said.

"Or the *Summer Workbooks*," Annie put in.

"And we'll be on our way," Pete said.

"Well," Mrs. Pete said, "after we drop the keys off with that man at the Little Hotel."

We were going home; we'd make it home in time for our eighth birthday.

We can't say we were cheerful, not at the idea of

spending our first birthday ever without Mommy and Daddy. What a significant birthday to spend without them — the Eights turning eight!

But we were cheered.

* * * * * * * *

"Ninety-nine boxes of juice on the wall, ninety-nine boxes of juice!"

Somehow, the trip coming home was never half so fun or exciting as the trip going away.

"I know what we can do to liven things up," Pete said.

He did?

"We could stop at that roadside attraction over there!" Pete suggested enthusiastically when none of us responded.

"What's a roadside attraction?" Petal asked as we piled out of the Hummer.

"It's something on the side of the road," Jackie explained, "almost like a little museum of stuff you'd never get the chance to see at home."

"While you lot look at the roadside attraction," Pete said, "I need to go make a phone call. Back in a tick!"

Huh. We wondered who he'd gone to call so quickly and why he couldn't use the phone in the Hummer.

"So what's this roadside attraction about?" Durinda asked.

"It says that it's a snail farm," Marcia said, reading the little sign.

"My, that looks lively," Rebecca said. "Are any of them even moving?"

* * * * * * * *

"Fifty-three boxes of juice on the wall, fifty-three boxes of juice!"

Wow, we realized. That could get old quickly.

"Time for another roadside attraction," Pete said, "and another phone call."

"Who do you think he's calling?" Marcia wondered.

"And why doesn't he just use our car phone to do it?" Georgia wondered further.

We shrugged.

"What's this roadside attraction for?" Zinnia asked.

"I hope it's not another snail museum." Petal shuddered. "That last one was almost too much excitement for my delicate heart. I nearly fainted."

"Oh, look," Durinda said. "It's a combination museum. On one side, it's a museum of unusual buttons, while on the other, it's a museum of unusual kitchen appliances."

"I'll bet," Rebecca said, "our family could make a better roadside attraction."

* * * * * * * *

All those stops for roadside attractions and one more phone call on Pete's part — as it turned out, the trip back was far longer than the trip out had been.

We arrived back at 6:00 a.m. on August 8, exactly two hours before the official beginning moment of our eighth birthday, 8:00 a.m. being the time Annie was born, with the rest of us being born a minute apart for the next seven minutes.

But that was all okay, because we were home.

Home.

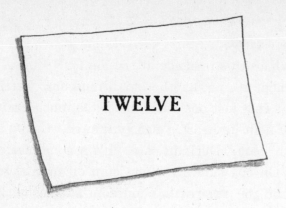

TWELVE

But what was that banner doing draped across our front door? That banner that read—we squinted our eyes against the early-morning light—in tall, rainbow-colored letters . . .

HAPPY BIRTHDAY, EIGHTS!

It hadn't been there when we left home six days ago. We were almost certain we would have noticed it. Had Carl the talking refrigerator and robot Betty somehow done this? But, we thought, Carl couldn't walk, and Betty's handwriting was never this neat.

"Surprise!" Will Simms shouted, coming around the house from one side.

"Surprise!" Mandy Stenko shouted, coming around the house from the other side.

"Happy birthday, Eights!" the McG and the Mr. McG shouted, coming from wherever such people come from.

"Surprise!" Will and Mandy and the McG and the Mr. McG and the Petes yelled all together.

"You did this," Zinnia said, turning to Pete. "You called them all from the road."

"Well, yes," Pete admitted, "but the missus helped me come up with the idea."

We were relieved he'd stopped calling her Mrs. Pete and was back to calling her the missus.

"Now let's go inside," Pete said, herding us along. "I suspect there are presents and a great big cake waiting for you in there."

* * * * * * * *

The cake waiting for us was big and it was great too; the rainbow lettering on it said *Happy Birthday Annie, Durinda, Georgia, Jackie, Marcia, Petal, Rebecca, Zinnia!*

We were grateful for that cake, the bigness and greatness of it, and we were doubly grateful that they'd spent the extra money to have all of our names spelled out rather than simply settling for the easier *Happy Birthday, Eights!* Seeing those separate names spelled out like that — it did make each of us feel special.

But we were too excited to open presents and eat cake, too excited from everything that had happened in the past week and everything that was going on. Besides, it wasn't our official birthday yet and wouldn't be until the big clock in the drawing room struck eight.

So instead of opening presents or eating cake, we spent a good bit of time filling in Will and Mandy and the McGs on what we'd been up to on our vacation.

"And then there was no room at the inns," Durinda said, proceeding to tell about that part.

"And then Annie made us do *Summer Workbook*," Georgia said, proceeding to tell about that part.

We could see the McGs were both pleased and impressed about that part.

"And then I caught a shadow following me," Petal said, "that everyone thought was my shadow but that turned out to be a boy named George."

"And then," Zinnia said, "actually between some of that and before the rest of it, I called to the dolphins and they came and frolicked with me, with all of us."

Oh, Zinnia.

We stared at her, disappointed in her insistence in keeping on with her fiction, particularly since company had come to call.

She stared back at us, clearly disappointed in our unwillingness to go along with her fiction.

"What?" she said, continuing to stare.

It was odd, how wounded and innocent she looked at that moment.

"Oh, fine," Zinnia said when no one else spoke. "I'm sick of people not believing me, never having faith in me." She paused. "Zither!" she called.

Zither came trotting in.

What was Zinnia doing? we wondered. Was she going to pretend she could talk to one of the cats again?

It was such an old trick; tired, really.

The other cats meandered in, so when Zinnia headed for the front door, Zither by her side, there was a rather large troop of humans and cats trailing behind them.

Where was Zinnia going? we wondered. Was she so angry, angry over our perfectly reasonable and understandable behavior, she was going to run away from home? Or pretend to, like she pretended she could talk to cats and a few other animals?

We watched, rather curiously we will admit, as Zinnia and Zither stepped over the threshold and out a few steps onto the front lawn. In fact, we were so curious, we crowded behind closely, forming an arc around them.

So we were there to see it when Zinnia looked to the sky and nodded slightly. Suddenly there came the sound of thunder, and a greater variety of birds than we'd ever imagined existed filled the whole sky overhead.

Before we could take in what we were seeing, Zinnia leveled her gaze at the street in front of us and then at the woods around us, and she nodded her head again.

And then came all manner of animals imaginable: cats and dogs and bunnies, to be sure, but also larger animals, like lions and tigers and bears and giraffes and kangaroos and pandas and strange animals we didn't even have names for, all of them filling our entire lawn.

We would have been scared, but we were too busy being awed, even Petal.

We were suddenly sure that, if there'd been an ocean nearby, Zinnia could have summoned all the creatures of the sea as well.

"Wow," Georgia whispered in Rebecca's general direction. "When we warned you that you'd better not keep teasing Zinnia about her thinking she could talk to the cats, because who knew what might happen if she really could talk to them, I never imagined it would turn out like this."

Rebecca gulped.

The truth is, none of us had imagined this. None of us *could* have imagined this.

But we should have. We saw that now.

Zinnia was right. We'd never believed what she said, never had faith in her. But we should have. For in the final analysis, what were the options? Zinnia, our sister, had claimed she could communicate with animals. We thought this meant that she was either lying — and we'd never had any other evidence that Zinnia was a liar — or crazy — and we'd never had any other evidence that Zinnia was crazy. That left only one option, really: Zinnia was telling the truth, and she'd been telling the truth all along.

We should have believed her from the start.

We should have had faith.

"Do you believe me now?" she asked quietly without turning around.

We nodded silently. Even though she couldn't see us, we were sure she got the message.

"Does anyone want to check the loose stone in the drawing room?" Zinnia asked, her back still to us.

We shook our heads. We didn't. We knew what any note now would say: that we were a bunch of big fat idiots. Zinnia had had her power all her life, had always known it without needing to be told she had it. It had taken us that long to get wise.

"I'll admit," Zinnia admitted quietly, turning to face us at last, "I always knew I could do . . . *things,* but even I never knew I could do something so large."

Then Zinnia turned, facing forward again, and nodded her head one more time.

All the animals on the lawn parted, creating a path, and one last animal proceeded down that path toward us.

"What is it?" Marcia asked.

"It looks like a horse," Petal said, staring at the snow-white creature, "with a great big horn on its head."

"I don't think it's a horse," Jackie said.

"It's a unicorn," Zinnia informed us in a hushed voice, "the last of its kind in the whole world."

On any other day prior to this one, we might not have believed Zinnia.

But on this day we did.

This really was wonder.

We watched as the unicorn swayed the last few steps to where Zinnia stood, and that's when we noticed the saddle across its back. To the riderless saddle was attached a satchel.

Saddle, satchel—we were tempted to try to say that five times fast but we refrained from doing so.

"Oh," Zinnia said mildly, reaching to take an item sticking out from the satchel, "the unicorn must be here to bring me my gift."

On any other day, we might have doubted her certainty. But not on this one. We might have suggested going to the drawing room to look behind the loose stone so we could see if there was a new note there informing us that Zinnia's gift had arrived, congratulating her, and telling us all in general that there were now sixteen down and zero to go.

But we didn't need to do that. We knew what we were looking at.

We gathered closer around Zinnia to inspect the object she was holding in her hands. The way she held it, turning it this way and that—it was as though it weighed hardly anything at all. The object was a round glass ball sitting on a golden base. Attached to the top of the ball was a tiny circle, and attached to that was a metal hook.

"A Christmas ornament in the shape of a snow globe!" Zinnia said with glee. "I've always loved snow globes!"

It seemed an odd gift for a person to receive: a Christmas ornament in August.

But we didn't think any more of that as we gathered closer still, seeing what Zinnia was seeing: the pretty glass; the stone house within, which despite its miniature size somehow looked practically as big as a mansion but not quite and yet still slightly larger than our own home; the tower room, so similar to ours, jutting out from the top.

Zinnia shook the ornament then, making the glittery dust fly all around the sort-of mansion.

"Wait a second," Zinnia said, peering closer at the ornament. "It looks like there's a person waving his arms, leaning out of the tower window."

Zinnia looked even closer.

We all did.

We *knew* that man, that tiny man who was waving his arms wildly at us.

"Daddy?" Zinnia said.

CPSIA information can be obtained
at www.ICGtesting.com
Printed in the USA
FSHW012219100519
58041FS

Benefit of the Debt

Endorsements

"There are times I pick up a manuscript or a book and peruse a chapter or two and sense that a wonderful person spent months and likely years crafting the message they are sharing. Then there are rare times that I have the distinct privilege to take a peek at a manuscript that both gives me a glimpse inside the heart of an honest, real and passionate writer as well as a better understanding of our loving Father. The book you are holding reflects the second description. I don't know Meg Miller, however I know, love and am sold out for Jesus and am cheering from my study as I see more than transparency in Meg's book... I see the vulnerability of a woman who surrendered her agenda, her rights and her pride to be open with God and to allow Him the place He desires in our hearts... full bore brokenness.

Meg has penned a book that will mess with you. That's why I'm cheering her on... it's real and honest and more than transparent... it's *vulnerable*.

If you want a great marriage then read, pore over, and allow our loving and forgiving Father to shed both insight and freedom in your life."

–Dr. Gary Rosberg,
Co-founder & CEO, America's Family Coaches, Author *Guard Your Heart & Healing the Hurt in your Marriage*

"In a day when betrayal through pornography seems all too commonplace, many couples struggle with not only the 'why' but also the *'how'* of getting through it. In sharing her own raw and surprising story, Meg Miller opens an insight that could be a key for others in finding healing and hope in the midst of the pain."

–Pat Jones, Lead Pastor,
Eastern Hills Wesleyan Church

———————————

"Honestly, most of the preaching and teaching about sex, lust and porn is not getting the job done. In Benefit of the Debt, Meg Miller, tells a very compelling story of her life and what God has taught her about herself when it comes to real love, true forgiveness, moving on and overcoming! Anyone who has suffered betrayal, loneliness and loss will find a kindred spirit in these pages. Meg tells you how to find beauty and fulfillment in the ashes of life. Her unique perspective makes this book a must read for women — and men."

–Wes and Claudia Dupin,
founding pastors of <u>Daybreak.tv</u>, author of "Almost Chosen"

Benefit of the Debt

*How my husband's porn problem ~~ruined~~
saved our marriage*

MEG S. MILLER

ELITE

Xulon Press
2301 Lucien Way #415
Maitland, FL 32751
407.339.4217
www.xulonpress.com

E^{xulon}LITE

Printed in the United States of America.

ISBN-13: 978-1-54562-960-4

Foreword

I n a spiritual formation class, we work on how Christians can get victory over sin as a part of their spiritual growth. To start the unit I ask students to list the sins *Christians face most today*. They list four sins immediately:

- Internet Porn
- Pride
- Lust
- Anger

Then they pause... they run out of sins. These four get listed quickly each time. In fact I've come to call them the "foul four" sins. Then students run out of gas and just sit there, thinking.

At the pause I usually ask, "OK, for each sin on our list, let's decide as a class whether men or women are *more inclined* to this sin." In all my classes they've agreed: while women are sometimes tempted in these areas, men are more inclined to these four sins.

So I say, "Only women participate now—decide among your-selves what four sins you'd add to the list that you think *women* are more inclined toward. Silence. Furrowed brows. Thinking. A long pause.

Really! Each time the women who (along with the men) had quickly offered the "foul four" are at a loss to quickly add "besetting sins" that women seem more inclined toward.

And now for the part that got me.

The last two times I did this activity the women unanimously agreed on what they considered *the chief besetting sin of women*:

• Lack of self esteem

I'm serious. So were they. The last two times I did this when a woman offered "Self esteem" the entire group of women audibly responded, "Yeah—that's it!"

You see where I'm headed? To the men in the class these co-eds were saying, *"While you men struggle with pornography, lust, pride and anger we women struggle with not thinking highly enough of ourselves."* (Several men in the class always visibly roll their eyes.)

To be fair, the women (after considerable time) finally add three other sins: *resentment, bitterness,* and *lack of trust.* But even their expanded list appears to the guys in the class that men struggle with really destructive sins while women fight minor sins. This male response was actually summed up the last time I did this. One male student exclaimed, "Gee, if I just struggled with those sins I'd be a saint!" To him "women's temptations" were misdemeanors while his own besetting sins were obviously capital crimes.

So, it got me thinking. Are men really more inclined to sin than women—are they somehow in the grip of original sin more than women? Can this be true? In much of the ancient world women were considered weaker moral creatures with a greater inclination to sin than males—has this been reversed in the modern world?

Or, have we labeled "male sins" crimes while mislabeling the temptations of women as less severe?

Or, are female college students just more unaware of their sin than males?

Now, I know that dealing with sin and gender differences is touchy territory—all generalizations have exceptions and are not always true (or they would not be generalizations). But I keep sensing that my students are uncovering something interesting. What is it? What are they discovering about themselves, the church culture or theology?

In 2005, I posed these questions to my own readership. Twelve years later, someone has finally provided a satisfactory answer: Meg S. Miller, the author of this book.

Women might not like this book but Meg has scraped one huge scab on many of today's marriages.

It will be hard reading for many women but Miller's gripping story and discoveries could be the lifeline to many marriages that are falling apart. It's a modern day millennial's story of one woman facing the prophet Nathan as he says "You are the man." Only this time he says, "You are the woman."

If you want a book about how to fix your erring husband don't get this book. It is about fixing yourself.

Miller's telling her story in everyday chatty street-talk makes this book a gripping page-turner. Here she serves as a modern millennial prophet with good aim. She aims right into the center of your own heart, not your husband's.

This book *will* make some women mad. But it will save many other marriages.

–Keith Drury
Professor Emeritus, Indiana Wesleyan University

Table of Contents

Without a Debt

When we got married, my husband and I knew we would
have some baggage. We knew there would be problems.
After all, that's what everyone tells newlyweds, right? "Brace yourself, it's not easy," they said. And even *they* had no idea the crap we
were bringing into the covenant with us.

Even the most successful wives gave me that semi-sad look on
my wedding day, the look of someone who had accepted the per-
manency of slavery. And yet, these successful wives weren't slaves. I
knew them personally and even looked up to them for their cunning
and resourcefulness. Yes, even for their kindness toward their men.
So what was the cryptic sadness in there?

Nevertheless, I was ready. Anything would have been better
than loneliness (right?). I was even prepared for the whole sexual
weirdness that they say "all men" bring to a marriage. The lust thing.
People had tried to explain it, and I heard a few mentions of it in
church, but of course nothing can prepare a young wife for the
revelation of porn in her house that first time. So I knew my husband would struggle, as they say. I even thought I was ready for it.
Granted, I wasn't the prettiest girl in the bunch, but I could hold
my own in a crowd. I couldn't compete with the porn stars, but at

1

least I was as good as he could do in real life. So what did I have to fear? He knew better than to cheat, so I felt safe.

Until the day I found it.

We had been married for three years, and I supposed that was just too much for him to handle. It turns out he was a weakling after all, I thought. Just another piece of crap dude who couldn't keep his act together. Creep. Loser. Smallish. I'd probably catch him breathing hard at random times if I paid close enough attention. Yuck. Needless to say, I was disgusted and repulsed.

But the weird thing was my devastation. The power of my hurt alarmed me. You may be familiar with this feeling. I felt a certain surprise at the power of the hurt. I mean, obviously, everyone knows that a wife will feel stung when she finds these things, but it was more than a sting; it was a finishing blow. It took me completely by surprise.

I went to a support group for women whose men were dealing with "sexual brokenness"—pervs, pretty much, the lot of them. Freaks and screwups. Yet their wives—the women in the support group—were all so sweet to me. The first night I went, there were about ten women in the room, sitting around a table, with one leader. All of their stories were horrible. Most of the husbands represented had acted out their fantasies, but a few of us had men with *only* the "porn thing." I remember sitting in that room, starving physically because I had started such a strict diet since I found those images. I was determined to get thinner. My husband and I had been going to counseling for three months when our counselor finally convinced me to attend this weekly women's thing for the first time. So there I was. Starving, listening, and crying.

I didn't say a word through that first meeting because I couldn't stop crying. I wasn't crying for me alone but for all of this mess and how sad the whole world is because of men and their horse crap sexual sin. It wasn't just the browsing history at home, although that was cry-worthy. But also the women in sex slavery, the kids without fathers, the wives who "found out" that day, the wives who never will, the people who have to work those cameras, and the kids who see too much too early, the whole industry. All of it. I cried and cried.

You don't even realize how idealistic you are as a wife until you find something. You really have no idea how much you look to your husband for sustenance until he gets his kicks elsewhere. And that was me.

I was so surprised at the sight of my crumpled-up self, sobbing. Who was this?

The second meeting, hungrier than ever, I managed to say my name when we all introduced ourselves, but I couldn't say more than that. I had nothing to say. Only tears. It was as though someone had died. I couldn't explain it. Here was a room full of women whose guys had done much uglier stuff, but I'm the one sobbing. They had kids and lawyers involved. My story was pretty small compared to theirs. So what was my problem? It was as though my dreams of a faithful husband (and subsequently a happy life) were shattered, and all the guy had done was check out some boobs on the computer. Granted, he had a porn problem. But still, what was wrong with me? How could this have sent me into such a tailspin?

The only explanation lay in what I already knew: I had come to rely on my husband for things that only God could provide. Every book on "men and porn" told me that. Every woman in the room repeated it. But it hadn't *seemed* like he was on the throne of my life in

the daily grind. Heck, companionship was all I ever *really* needed from him. He had become quite distant with the stress of work and life. I don't even know what made me check the computer. I truly had no suspicions—only fear. And my fear was realized. It really didn't seem to me like I had idolized him. Looking back to the weeks and months before finding our browsing history, I tried to see where I may have been critical of him or harsh with my words. Like all wives, I could admit I'd been a wee bit nasty in my tone—on occasion. But was it enough to make him seek comfort with other women in his mind?

To this day, I still doubt that I *had* idolized him. In fact, the only thing that can convince me of my idolatry is the size of my pain when he was getting off with an image of someone else. I still doubt my ongoing tendency to expect more of him than I should. But always, that nagging reminder of my hurt repeats the truth: "Her desire will be for her husband..." (Genesis 3:16)

At that third meeting, I was able to tell the group my name and what I had found. That was progress. But I couldn't speak further than that. Again, tears thwarted my intent to share more. And again, when the tears stopped, I couldn't say anything because, wow, there really was nothing left to say. What could I say after all I thought was speakable had been proven a façade? And how could I say, "I feel this certain way" when five seconds later I would feel another way completely? I used to speak with such confidence, but now I didn't even know what was true or a lie.

I wanted to say, "My husband is repentant and willing to stop," but how did I know whether he really was? I wanted to say, "It's just pictures, he's never cheated," but how did I know that was true? Even today, how do I know he's presently faithful? How did I know he had

in fact joined a men's group specifically for this creepy stuff? How did I know he meant it when he said he was so sorry? What do you say in a support group when all you ever believed had been proven a lie?

I never was able to tell the group what was happening with my marriage or spiritual life. But after a few months of attending, I was able to ask questions. Many of the women were closer to God than any of the people I had met in my life. These women also claimed that they were at that moment closer to God than they had ever been before. This suffering was the best way, I saw, to get to know the Creator. And I could admit that that *did* sound nice. So I asked a lot of questions. God gave me the discernment to separate the bitter women from the healed, and I clung to those who told me of God, not men.

I don't know how women survive when they learn of their men's secret life and don't have a group like this. I dove into the book they recommended, a daily devotional (guide, really) for women who were going through this. Since I was still having trouble sleeping for all the thoughts and pain, I was able to get up early and talk to God alone. It was amazing. He comforted me. He assured me of His ability to make this right. And He promised me many things, like His commitment to always stay with me. Through His Word, I learned more about Him than I ever thought possible. And yet, it still hurt. Oh, every time I thought of it, I felt a stab. And I know you do, too.

During the time that I attended the women's group, there were a few glimmers of hope. There were a handful of times I realized it's possible to survive this. One was the day we discussed compassion for our husbands. We talked about the images we are all exposed to daily and discussed how strong the enemy's attacks are on our men. We talked about the wounds they received as children, and how lust acts

as a comfort to them and is not just a selfish hobby. My heart softened for my husband for the first time in months, and I went home and told him that I'm sorry for all the pressure he faces each day. I told him I am grateful for his willingness to fight for our marriage. It was still too early to tell whether he was serious with this commitment or not, but I still said it. In the next breath, I also told him that if ever I found another naked picture on our computer or anywhere else in our house, I was standing on the Word of God that grants me the blissful severance package of taking the kids with me when I left. Kids? Oh yes. That week, I had learned I was pregnant with our first of three.

I stopped dieting for the pregnancy and watched as my body grew into the opposite of what he wanted. No matter how he tried to assure me that I was his desire, the evidence against my "beauty" was in our browsing history. To this day, I do not believe that he would rather be intimate with me than with the women in his fantasy world. Let's get real. Even now you can't convince me that if he had a choice (and no consequences), he wouldn't choose Miss Airbrush. I can't compete with her.

Throughout the pregnancy, I kept going to the support group, which was like putting ointment on a burn. It was comforting to see those whose husbands were much "worse" than mine. It was comforting to pray together for God to be glorified and us to be restored. And it was comforting to get their perspectives on everything, from the new temptation to snoop all the way to the new enticement of flirting with other men. But comforting is not the same as healing. The comforting nuggets I got there could not compare with the healing I craved.

One night, I looked at all the faces there and realized that my man was "doing better" than all the other wives' husbands. There were other men who were repentant, but none so vocally and consistently as Joe, my husband. None attended a support group like Joe did or sought accountability the way he did. So I emailed the leader, seeking reassurance that I was still welcome:

Mrs. Adler,

I want badly to come on Wednesday nights, but I feel like this is a group for those who are in a phase where they need a group to recover. I hesitate to come and celebrate how well I'm doing (in Christ) or how well my husband is doing in his sobriety because I fear that some could be discouraged by comparing their situation to mine. However, I crave the community you've built, and I especially miss your own presence in my life. What are your thoughts on this?

I haven't told anyone else about Joe's thing yet. It's just too embarrassing, especially since they all know him as a leader in the church. So I'm feeling stuck. Our group might not identify with my journey (since it's "just porn"), and my friends couldn't possibly, since they don't even know.

I'm sure you've seen similar situations before. What do you recommend?

Thanks for everything. I am so grateful.

Megan

Her answer was this:

> You are right that most of the women who are
> attending are facing divorce and in most cases infi-
> delity. But there are a few newer women who are
> working on reconciliation with their husbands who
> are exhibiting repentance.
>
> Are you involved with a Bible study or
> small group?
>
> Love U!

"Well, shoot, there goes that lifeline," I realized. I was grateful that
Joe was doing well enough to get me kicked out of my own group,
but cripes, I was still a pile of steaming roadkill, needing help, while
my husband was fixing the car that hit me (if you will). The man
was on cloud nine. He looked forward to my tears because he was
acquiring the skills needed to comfort me. *His* support group didn't
kick him out for being "too healthy" but equipped him to grow.
So he was amazing. He told me every few hours how sorry he was
and how he truly never would do anything like that again. He told
me of small transgressions, such as how the ankles of a girl on the
metro commute caught his attention but he didn't check her out or
fantasize. He told me that he felt miserable when some long-haired
beauty caught his eye, and he did a double-take before he could con-
sult the Lord. The guy was a regular Ned Flanders. It made me sick.
Everything about him made me sick.

This went on for a year. I made little progress, and the pain
seemed just as fresh every day. You may be able to relate. I had

thoughts like: *What is my problem? Lots of women go through this and survive. Why am I such a wreck? Am I a* needy *woman?* Before this whole thing, I had prided myself on being the antithesis of a clingy wife. In fact, my career was soaring. Applause and recognition followed me around all day in the office. We had spent a few weeks in the Bahamas, all expenses paid (plus a generous stipend) with my company. We partied day and night there. Anyone would have loved living my life, but I was miserable with this injury to my spirit. Why did my Achilles heel seem to have done more than cripple my heart? Indeed, I was dying from this thing. What was my problem?

I asked God these questions, and for many months, I seemed to get silence in response. I thought God was so cruel not to give me answers to these questions. After all, I was doing the right thing: *focusing on my emotional problems* instead of trying to change my guy. Right? God should be admiring me! He should be fixing the hurt and holding me up as an example to other women. But instead, all I got was silence.

Now, let me pause here to say that I was misguided, but I did one thing right during this time: I pressed into that silence. I begged God not to leave me to my emotions but to answer my questions about why this whole thing *still* hurt so much. Was I defective? I spent many mornings yelling at God, "Answer me! What is my problem? Why can't I get over this? Why does it hurt quite like this? What is the deal? Is there hope for healing? Have all the other women just learned to live with it?"

Indeed, that's the best explanation that I could come up with as I desperately observed other "survivors" in my life. My pastor's wife. The attendees of my support group. And even the leader. I gathered

that they had just learned how to live with the terrible pain. And now that I consider it, it's probable that they *have* merely learned to live with this thorn in their sides. It's possible that they live every moment thinking that this martyrdom is their "lot in life," and that God must have something happy for them on the other side of eternity since marriage is a huge disappointment. I knew that I had the choice to believe that, too, but the implications sucked. How would I ever enjoy sex again if I knew I was with a creepy porn freak who didn't deserve me and my chaste ways? Heck, I didn't even *think* about sex with other dudes, let alone crave it or fantasize about it.

In fact, reverse the roles for a moment: How lame would *Joe* have to be if I were to need constant prayer and accountability just to keep my attention on him? And may I pause here to include a few honest thoughts I had about his trysts with his fake women? I was jealous of him. I wanted some "escape" from daily life, too—one which stayed in my mind and nobody else needed to know about. One which could be easily conjured up as well as quickly put away. I wanted a little shot of fun on occasion for myself. I wanted to "struggle" with lust so that it could give me an out every once in a while. I even had one-on-one lunches with a few male co-workers to try to "get mine."

But try as I might, I just never sensed a longing for the attentions of other men the way I wanted my husband's loyalty. If I were to put the two side-by-side (that is, the attentions of other guys versus Joe's complete loyalty), then Joe's loyalty would always rule in my heart. I desired it. I needed it. I wanted to be the only woman he ever craved. And when I view the two side-by-side, I realize one was within my power to achieve (the attentions of other men) while

the other was dead forever. Ruined. So perhaps, I reasoned, I desire the one only because it's the one I cannot have—"the grass is always greener" kind of thing. That was my problem. This was a conclusion I reached that never completely satisfied me. It worked at night, and I was able to sleep. But in the morning, I was hurting again, and I had to admit that no true healing had come.

Oh, how I craved healing. I still remember how it tortured me, that thirst to get well. You could even say—I lusted for it.

Seeds of Debt

O ne day, I was reading a story of Jesus in the Bible where a blind social outcast begged Jesus to have mercy on him. The Lord neared the man and asked him, "What do you want me to do for you?" (Luke 18)—as though He couldn't see the man was suffering from his blindness and diminished status. This struck me. Was Christ being cruel?

Incidentally, I have a friendship with this Christ, and I have gotten to know Him a bit. Cruelty, sarcasm, and even mere insensitivity would be so uncharacteristic that I decided to meditate on the situation for a few minutes. I asked Him what He was doing by asking a blind person what He could do for him.

Obviously, if I were astute, I'd have put myself in the blind man's position and explored how I would have answered that question. And instead of blindness, this gaping wound that plagued my every moment would be my "thing." Was God asking me what I wanted? Seriously? Was it possible that the first answer in my mind was not true? Because what I *wanted* was my husband's loyalty and steadfast love. I was not asking for a weekend in Paris. I just wanted the guy to stop messing around with other women in the safety of his mind.

"Please," I begged.

"Really?" God asked me.

"Well, yeah, really." Cripes, this conversation was ridiculous. The blind man wants eyesight, and I want this. It's not complicated.

"Nothing more? Nothing deeper? Nothing in you?"

I understood where He was going. What if I had the ability to ask God to change *me?* What would I change? Well, I wouldn't be such a hot mess over the whole thing. I would want Him to make me stronger, more independent, and less needy. "Make me cool, God." Less hurt.

So there. Change me. That's fine. Whatever. I didn't care. If God wanted to heal me through making Joe great, well then that would be my vote. But if He wanted to change *me* into someone who wouldn't be such a wreck over sexual sin, well, then fine, do it; that'll do. Get to work, God, make it happen, whatever. I'm in. Even if it hurts. Sure, everyone says "pruning" will hurt. That's fine, let's get on with it. Go. Change me.

But instead, two days later, something wild happened.

I was driving on the Capital Beltway, listening to my everyday sermon on XM Radio. The speaker was talking about suffering. It had been over a year since I found my husband's stash of nudie pictures on our computer, and yet I still reached to turn up the volume. I always did. If it regarded suffering, I needed it. I was desperate for it. *"What will this pastor say? Please help me . . . it still hurts so much . . . God speak right now. God, say something this time. God, Do something for once. I'm still so messed up from his porn/lust thing!"*

And God? Silent. It was the worst. So I continued, talking aloud to God over the radio preacher.

"And if You want to bring healing to me by changing me instead of my guy, I'm ready. I'll do whatever You tell me. Even if it is something deeper than making me stronger."

My story breaks down here. This is where things become surreal. I sensed God near, and He whispered something into my heart—a mere suggestion. A whiff of a thought. And this suggestion that God offered sounded to me like a complete change of subject.

Immediately, the world tilted, and the car in front of me slammed on its brakes. I have a hard time believing it myself, but my own brakes failed at that moment, and I swerved to barely miss the car in front of me. The car in my *new* lane honked and swerved to avoid me, and my radio—no lie—my radio volume began to creep *up*. My engine casually died, as though it was just minding its business, and I frantically worked to pull the vehicle back under control. Still in motion, I slammed in the clutch and cranked the motor. I had slowed and was traveling at about thirty miles per hour, with no power steering. It took every ounce of my arms' strength to pull over, coast to a stop on the shoulder and assess.

WHAT. THE. EFF. Cars whizzed by, rocking my stalled vehicle threateningly. A few times I thought they were buzzing close just to make the point that I'd chosen a bad spot. My hands were shaking, and I reached to restart the car, but stopped. There was a lingering voice that told me not to ignore the fact that the Almighty had given me a new concept just as things began to *freakishly* malfunction. I needed to catch it before I lost it from memory completely. So I sat and probed my spirit.

God. God, I'm here. Please repeat yourself. Please don't let me lose Your message. I got a taste of something, just a hint of what You said, but I really didn't "hear" You. I need You to repeat Yourself, please. Please. I've suffered toward it for so long. I've been reaching for this very point; I'm sure of it. I'm starving for it, and there's only one thing I know for certain: without it, whatever it is, I'll live another ho-hum dull "Christian" life with no real joy. The kind where I learn to cope. I don't want to cope. I want to change. I want *Your* change. I know that what You just implied in my heart is what will heal me. It's what I've been looking for. So what was it?

Since I knew a little bit about God's personality from meeting with Him before, I sensed He was hesitant to illuminate the message He had for me. He seemed to go back and forth with me.

"Are you sure you want this, Meg?"

"My God, my God, it's *all* I want. I must be healed of this pain."

"But Megan, this might hurt your heart more than the pornography did."

"But God, it's from *You*, so it *must* be good for me."

"You don't realize what you're asking Me for."

"No, but I know You and have seen Your ways are far higher than my own or my husband's or my preacher's or my support group's ways. You're far ahead of the self-help books and the other authors who claim to know how to heal from this. You must not abandon me to this misery."

"But Meg this will change you forever. You'll never be the same."

"I'm begging You, Father, give it to me—I will not stop asking until You make this clear to me. I want to change. I want to be well again regardless of the behavior of others. You planted a suggestion in my heart a few minutes ago on this busy road. Give it to me clearly now. For Your sake. Because I know You have already done the irreversible. You cannot ungive what You've already begun to give me. Either I explore this new idea on my own or You join me and give me insight."

And then it became immediately obvious. And it was more terrible than He ever could have prepared me for.

The answer that God finally gave me that day was an image or, rather, a series of images. The first image was a glimpse of my husband's heart, wounded just as badly as mine was. Immediately, I felt compassion for him. Or rather, I felt compassion for *this image of him*, since of course Joe's real heart was *not as damaged as mine* was. Nobody's heart was quite as bruised as mine. After all, that's the whole reason for my crying out—something was amiss with my heart to be so messed up. However, this first image of Joe's heart, equally injured, haunted me. Anybody in this much pain would certainly receive my empathy. God pressed the image onto my mind as though He wanted it to stick.

"A mere suggestion, just a hint. But I want it to stay. It matters," He whispered. "Stay with Me..." so I did.

I turned my mental eyes back to Joe's ill-treated heart, and I forced myself to consider it. Where did the supposed wounds come from? I had heard that porn hurts guys, and so do the lies and compromises they make. I had heard that the temptation alone hurts

them. But this was all horse crap. I didn't want to hear it again, and I sensed that God was dismissing those things as well. What else did he have in his life that could hurt him so badly? His job? He didn't even care too much about his job. His farming background? Perhaps that was it. Perhaps moving to DC with me to start a family had wounded him as badly as his transgressions had hurt me.

Yet this conclusion also felt lacking. My mental eyes scanned the parts of Joe's life one by one until my own role came into focus. Sure, I was guilty of criticizing the guy on occasion, just like every involved wife. I moved on. Instantly, I sensed God's gentle hand turning me back to look again on myself.

"Okay," I said reluctantly. "I'll examine myself again." I had done this a hundred times before. After all, this was the main point of most of the self-help books on the topic. "OK, God, let's look at Megan as the source of Joe's horrific wounds, theoretical as they are." Mind you, I'm still on the side of the road as rush-hour traffic shoves my vehicle side-to-side, again and again. "Show me, God. Show me how I could have inflicted *that* much hurt on a guy guilty of the porn thing." I was like a teenager rolling her eyes as she begins the task of cleaning her nasty room for the zillionth time. I'm ashamed to say I was mouthing the word *fine* as I grudgingly returned my attention to myself as culpable for the dude's supposed pain.

Now, remember: these are all *hypothetical* images from the Lord. He was merely *suggesting I consider* what it would *look like* if I were the cause of Joe's heart being so hurt. God quietly asked me "Since these are all hypothetical and you're not responsible for any of the images, why don't we look a little closer at what your daily life would look like if the 'made-up allegations' were true?" It sounded safe to

me, so I took His hand and entered the next image: it was a scene where the players, Joe and I, were tackling everyday tasks. Both of our wounded hearts were on display. Joe was trying on new shoes. I saw the make-believe Megan suggest Joe not wear the shoes outside in the mud in case we wanted to return them. Right away a new wound appeared in Joe's heart.

My (real) world shifted beneath me again as I tried to grasp the enormity of this suggestion. Had God just showed me that my good-intentioned (and arguably well-reasoned) proposal to Joe had *hurt* him? And that every similar suggestion that I had offered Joe for the last five years—was destructive? This was insane. It was laughable. It still is, as I imagine the depiction God gave me.

"You can*not* suggest that my everyday assistance to the man is damaging. You cannot." And yet He did.

"Am I responsible for the dude's oversensitivity?" I asked God.

"We are only responsible for ourselves," He replied.

"Sweet. Then even *if* Joe's heart is as hurt as I am, and even *if* it is because of my daily interactions with him, then You are telling me that he is responsible for his being so hurt."

"Keep your eyes on your own obligation. To really achieve healing, we must only focus on what Megan is responsible for."

I knew that healing is what I desperately wanted. I had abandoned the thought of changing my man or even hoping for his restoration. Once I jumped ship on ever hoping for Joe to love me without any extra mental images, and once I told God that I would live with a husband who never kicked the habit in exchange for His healing in my heart, it seemed God began to move.

Since God was stressing my own responsibility, I clung to the task like a lifeboat in shark-infested waters. If you have ever really heard directly from God Himself, you know the feeling, and it doesn't matter what He's saying; you just don't want Him to stop. Just hearing from Him—He could have been telling me about the weather forecast, I didn't care—it was enough to change my life.

"Show me more," I said.

The next image appeared to me, and it was the picture of my supposed guilt, the very size and shape and magnitude of Joe's. Our hypothetical hearts were side-by-side now, and they were identical. My heart was damaged from his sexual sins, and his heart was damaged from my daily words and demeanor.

And not just "damaged." His heart was *every bit as hurt as* mine was. That is a huge difference between the lessons I had been taught in churchy marriage books before.

I mean sure, every marital lesson I had learned kind of mentioned my tendency to get on the guy's case, but I never considered *my good-intentioned help* as "my Achilles' heel" in the same way his lust thing was his. I mean, really—my assistance to him has been as damaging as his unfaithful tendencies have been to me? The one thing so embedded in me that I couldn't imagine my life without it was now on display, but instead of an attribute, it was my greatest fault.

Beyond a Reasonable Debt

I was baffled. After all, my help was a mindset, not a sin, right?! Until this point I had thought my daily (aloud) assistance was improving the man's life. My very intellect, which I offered almost hourly to my husband, seemed under attack by the One who gave it to me. This 180 was still impossible for me to grasp. After all, everything I said at home (mostly) was *sincerely* meant to help the dude. And if my intent was to help him by telling him how best to do things, and thus saving himself time/trouble/energy/money/whatever, then how could I be guilty of such a damaged heart in him? My motives were pure, even if my words occasionally had barbs.

Only now, God had shown me that my motives were not on trial. The source of Joe's hurt was on trial. And that source was me.

Everything—everything—in me raged against this proposed scenario. I was sick with desire to defend myself.

But to be that deeply connected with God that you can feel His breath on your cheek, and He reveals something this terrible and wild to you, means that you're already wide open. And when you're that exposed to Him already, it's not much crazier to acknowledge this: there's a microscopic part of you that knows these things are true.

Since the hearts and guilt that day were still theoretical, and God hadn't *really* charged me with anything, I was free to walk around and explore this new image. Every angle was interesting and terribly relevant to me. In the middle of my spitting anger, I had to admit: if God's experiment in "what if" had any truth to it, well, then, that would explain a lot. You see, half of my "porn problem" was from confusion—there were so many new questions about how the world *really* works, how anyone on earth could be happy, who Joe really is (faithful?), and who I really am (worth a fight?).

And if God's proposed scenario were true, a good number of those questions would now have answers.

For starters, it would explain the phenomenon of men and their sex-sin accountability groups, while women have identified nothing of an "equal and opposite" nature. Meaning, if God wants to suggest that we have our own Achilles heel the way men tend toward sexual sins, well then what would ours be? I know you're tempted, like I was, to name a few general sins like sloth or selfishness *or even criticism* as our sins, but nothing comes to a wife's mind, which is *just as widespread and just as tempting* and would make her *just as ugly and nasty* as a man and his disgusting sex crap.

Why does nothing come to mind for us? Or for those of us who try to offer the "female" sinful tendencies of discontentment or gossip, why do those never seem as prevalent as men and their sexual temptations? People often say that 99 percent of men struggle with lust. Why do people rarely say that 99 percent of women criticize their men? Or even if preachers and authors and philosophers *do say* that 99 percent of women are critical, then why isn't it treated as despicably as men and *their* thing? Why can you hear a pin drop every time the porn

thing comes up in church, but when Rev wades into the vague criticism thing (addressing women), it's laced with zingers against men, opportunities for lighthearted chuckling, and even disclaimers that this "sometimes" affects "a few women among us?"

The answer is because self-righteousness by nature is impossible to detect in oneself. Impossible. And if someone points it out to you, it, by its very nature, it is impossible to take as seriously as it ought. No other pitfall has this characteristic. None.

The more I thought about it, the more I realized I have been duped into thinking that men have sexual sins, and women have— um—women have—seriously, what do women struggle with to the same degree? Sins of gossip? Sure, but I've never seen a gossip accountability group in a church. Sorry, but I've seen thousands of men's sex groups. What is the one thing that should have women running to accountability groups more than any other temptation? We're all over the place. Lying? Sure, some women lie a lot (well, I used to fib hourly), but it's not a lifelong struggle that 99 percent of women can admit feeling. Even the sin of a critical spirit is something all women acknowledge as a little side note in their lives without sensing the need to go through a twelve-step program to uproot.

That, of course, would be ridiculous. Or would it?

What if God never let us off the hook that easily and instead, gently led us back toward the original question to start over? What would we come up with? Would we ever arrive at our desire to see our husbands improve as a huge sin? If not (the way we have not yet so far), that would explain the lack of support and accountability groups for women in their "Achilles' heel" area. Would it not?

In fact, let's go a step further: It's offensive to consider (innocent women being so culpable of such hurt, that is), so we do not go there as a church. Visit this idea with me: What if—just *what if* God were onto something here, and we entertained the concept that this is our "thing" the way sexual sin is men's "thing." The churches should then be full of women's groups *committed* to constantly discussing and attacking this topic.

But we don't. It's a mere chapter in each marriage book, not the whole thing. It'll never rise to that level. You know why? Because women, in a what-came-first-the-chicken-or-the-egg situation, *laugh* at the thought of their help being hurtful, especially if it's brought up by a guy. Imagine a church with groups like that, devoted to uprooting the accidentally critical heart in its women, an ongoing group that meets often and never changes topics. Then envision with me that same church has a *support group for the men* who are "healing" from their wives' words. Imagine a support group for men whose wives have been trying to change them each day under the guise of assistance, most of the time without even realizing it.

May I suggest the men may find genuine support and healing at this place? May I suggest leaders simply consider the subversive nature of this idea? And do you have what it takes to explore in your own mind *why* this image is so ridiculous? Remember again the support group I went to at the beginning of my story. What's the men's version of that group?

Answer me.

If you have no answer, then do you mean to suggest there is no *men's version*? If God wants to open the Church to imagining that we wives have an equal and opposite (not just similar and adapted)

indulgence that kills marriages, then I imagine He would also like to see an equal and opposite investment to care for the people coping with that hurt.

But no way. Talk about shame. No man would want to be in that group. You know why? Because they doubt their own heart's damage. We can go to a support group for women who have been subjected to men's horribleness without much shame because, after all, we didn't do anything wrong, correct?

But men can't, because too often, we have convinced them we're not hurting them. Or if we occasionally do admit to hurting them, at least we're using helpful tips to do it, not selfish sex hormones. In the same way we've "helped" them every day with what might be exposed as disapproving words, we have also used our words and demeanors to warn men not to go there and consider themselves very hurt. You know why?

It is because we have logic. Many times, they do not. After all, it is *logical* he should not wear his shoes outside if he's considering getting his money back for them. After all, it is *logical* he should engage with the children on occasion. And after all, it is *logical* to send a thank-you note to a business client after an important meeting. "I am *merely* assisting him by reminding him it's been a week," says the helpful wife.

Your head may be spinning, and that's because my best attempt to describe God's message to me will inevitably fall short. As He always does, he chose the scrawniest boy to fight a huge giant. Only this time, He's sending a halfwit kid to explain a divine phenomenon. If I could summarize, I'd remind you of the question that has always made me wonder: Why are men the only ones with a "main temptation" or "most common sin"? God's scenario suggested to

me they're *not* the only ones. If the female version of men's lust happened to be this (that our version of a marriage-killer is hourly "help" in the form of "indispensable" daily conversation), it would fill a gap I always wondered about, and it would mean we women are much less clean in all this pain than we could imagine.

Another way to phrase it is that when we think of sin, and God's forgiveness of it, we think of the bad things we did when we were young or angry or feeling lazy. We don't think of our list of achievements as sin, but this concept puts them in the same pile. All of it. Every bit of it needs forgiveness.

To me, this was a scandalous thought.

Always Had My Debts

So God's suggestion to me would finally answer (albeit uncomfortably and without much resolution) my greatest question about whether women have a female version of that one thing that all men "do."

But it would also clear up a few other things that had earlier sent me into such confusion as to feel vertigo. Here are ten paradoxical mysteries that would naturally come into focus if indeed God's message to me were true.

1. It would explain why we have not seen any female counterpart to the men's' sexual accountability groups in churches. We briefly considered this earlier, but clarity on this is more helpful than brevity. So let's dive back in.

Why would women join an accountability group for their attitudes if they believe, after all, that they're right? Or relatively clean? This one kills me. Someone has convinced us women that we have various little sins here and there, but nothing as hurtful as porn. That woman gossips, that wife exaggerates occasionally, or those moms don't serve in the church enough. That one brags, and that one laughs too much with her male co-workers. No one has considered

whether we have an *equal and opposing* force to the wayward sexual drive of husbands and their constant looking around. Or if they have, it's been a fizzle. I'm not saying we should program the healing, but if there were any indication in the Church that women have a grievous problem, there'd be a curriculum or two. Or a thousand. Because that's what Christians do when we're desperate to root something out. Instead though, we women study fluff, and lots of it.

Charles Swindoll said this:

> Let me mention one more "cheap substitute" so common among Christian wives in our day. It is learning about what's right rather than doing what is right . . . it has been my observation that a large percentage of Christian wives know more—much more—than they put into practice. And yet, they are continually interested in attending another class, taking another course, reading another book, going to another seminar . . . learning, discussing, studying, discovering . . . and what results? Normally, greater guilt. Or, on the other side, an enormous backlog of theoretical data that blinds and thickens the conscience rather than spurs it into action. Learning more truth is a poor and cheap substitute for stopping and putting into action the truth already learned.

And you know what? I'd heard a lot of Swindoll quotes but never this one. Somewhere along the way it got buried. What Swindoll

doesn't mention here is what knowledge does. First Corinthians 8:1 tells us it puffs up.

It puffs up. Knowledge puffs up the knowledgeable person. Please that I would never have all the right answers, or any of them, if that's the case. Because I've been there—I've been puffed up, and it's the worst. It really is.

This would explain why women are constantly looking for the next study or group or book. Men who struggle with lust (and let's be honest. If they say they don't, then they also might struggle with lying) are *aware* of their needs for improvement. Wives have no idea of their need. I get the sense that Christian women are constantly looking for the next "high" of being convicted but not *too* convicted. Because that's what these books/discussions/sermons deliver—a small shot of conviction. Women consume the material like termites and are immediately online signing up for the next conference. Is it possible they're deeply (subconsciously, even) searching for an end-all conviction, plus the absolution of it? Are they hoping to find themselves in a place of helpless abandon, faced with a pile of debt so high and wide that they cannot refute or fight or pay it? Something they cannot program or organize or serve their way out of? I'll be the first to raise my hand on this one. That was me, settling over and over again for a cheap substitute in the form of "gossip workshops" and "finding God in the chaos" books that convicted me of not having a stellar quiet time. Crap like that. Now I need to look no further than my own self—my very person—for a shot of conviction-with-gratitude.

Think about the "checklist" approach to self-improvement. "Do these three things, and nix those five habits, and your marriage

will be great," says every book on the shelf these days *and* every article on the topic *and* every sermon. Until we look at ourselves as the dirty culprits we are, responsible for the same measure of mutilation to our marriages as our husbands and their sins, we are dead in the water. No tactic can save us. In fact, our infatuation with these methods will continue to handicap our true healing by masking our need.

The truth is, we don't want to hear *from men* on what we could do better. I recently spoke with the head of marriage ministries at a mega church. He told me that he, of all people, would never be invited to speak at a women's conference or gathering. No man ever would. He would be most qualified, yet the invitation will never come. He would never have the ear of eager women, those who want desperately to know what they could do differently to improve their marriages. We just want quick bites, tips, ideas, nuggets. Not a complete rewiring. While many couples land in his office for counseling, no group of women has ever asked him to relay his side of the how-to-make-a-marriage-win story. We are simply not interested. We don't believe men understand where we're coming from. We flock to female speakers and female authors because at least they've been there. They can *encourage* us. Men have no idea what we go through. Right?

2. It would explain the spiral of deterioration we see when a guy seeks pictures or other pursuits for comfort while his wife seeks his behavioral change to comfort her. One feeds on the other, and the wife thinks she's merely vocalizing truth and help when, really, it's toxicity at its purest. And, of course, what does that poison do to

a man? It sends him to another source of comfort, which is *ahem* not always his wife.

If women are (by nature) as guilty as men, the result explains how marriage really is the "perfect storm" waiting to happen. Not only because men tend to wander in general, but because we tend to do our own equal amount of damage naturally. In our case, though, the damage is done with much less shame. It's that reduced shame that makes the perfect recipe for trouble, even more than if we both had tendencies that produced shame.

Women often feel self-righteous while men feel inadequate. Have you ever wondered why it can be so hard for men to simply be kind or generous? Why is it such a tall order? Why can't they just be faithful? Or honest? Why is it so hard for them to listen once in a while? Why do they have to have six screens within reach at all times? Why can't they at least roll down the window when they fart in the car? Do they purposely go around making a mess of everything as much as possible? If ever you resonate with any of these questions (or the tone behind them) even a little bit, you're guilty of the self-righteousness that God has shown me. You're awful. Now, mind you, I recognize it takes one to know one. In fact, to list these questions, I merely conjured up the most annoying things my husband does, so sure, you're awful, and I don't apologize for that because I know I'm even worse. I'd argue I'm a dozen times more self-righteous than the most oblivious woman. So what is the point of the mean old (above) questions? Is this a cute exercise? Or is it the very reason the American church has stopped almost all forward movement? What is the crux of God's message to women—the one realization that could get His people on the move again? Sure, God calls everyone to honesty and selflessness

and all that. But He's not calling on *you* to notice the lack thereof in your man. To do so is not cute. It's poisonous. And it may be our big thing, the one thing we all share.

3. With the spiraling deterioration still fresh in your mind, consider also his (and our) escalating needs. If my notion is true, it would explain this, too. Joe didn't need those images before our wedding. He just wanted me, even the flaws. And I didn't care about his skills as a roommate or spending habits before we got married. After all, we had love. Who needed perfect bodies (for him) and perfect behavior and performance (for me)? And in the beginning of this story, I mentioned that I didn't think I was requiring much of him, just companionship. At what point did we drift into needing these extreme things? I do remember our first year of marriage, wondering how he could do some things so inefficiently, but they didn't bother me to the point I felt the need to "help" (*criticize*) him, let alone fight. But day after day of the same "stupidity," and I couldn't help myself. I also couldn't imagine anyone asking me to keep quiet when my suggestions would clearly assist him.

A few moments ago I asked, "At what point did we drift into needing these extreme things?" I want to point out that at the time of the infraction, they don't seem extreme. He doesn't think a few fantasies here and there are going to mess us up too bad, and I couldn't believe it was good for me to stay silent when he caused a fender bender because he was texting. But on my wedding day I pledged not to mind if he was careless with the vehicles, and he thought it was not going to be a huge challenge to stay faithful. If the fault were upon him alone (like I had thought), then of course

our needs would escalate. And they did. If, on the other hand, we suddenly got a glimpse of how much hurt we had *both* inflicted on our marriage, then of course our entitlement (aka "needs") would *diminish*. And guess what. They have. Since that day on the beltway, I haven't needed my husband the way I once did.

When a guy looks at porn or fantasizes mentally, he's telling himself and you (and God) that his wife is not "cutting it" for him. He needs a little extra something. Just a couple clicks. Just a little wiggle room in the rules. A place to relax. And when you complain about never having help around the house, you're sending the same message: "I just need a little more out of this man." You tell yourself you're not asking for a weekend in Venice, just a few minutes of his time. Just some consideration. But look: it's the same message. "You're not cutting it for me, mister." I *just* need him to be on time. I *just* want him to care. I *just* deserve a break. Those little things are like him saying he doesn't need much, *just* a couple minutes online.

We're so hurt by that attitude of his needing a little more sexually. How then, can it be so radical that he'll be every bit as damaged from his wife's desire for x, y, or z? It's not. It's *not* crazy for him to be hurt. The crazy thing is that we've given men subtle warnings that remind them they're not *allowed* to be hurt.

Men feel unable to speak out on this topic while women are insanely vocal toward the condemnation of porn. Men cannot—dare not—go there with us. If their lust hurts us, and our criticism hurts them to the same intensity, then why don't we hear more about it? Where's the outcry? I can answer that for you: The lust battle has men and women screaming their heads off over the sheer evil of it. But only one or two brave chapters per marriage study even

touches on the topic of a woman's tendency to nag. The answer is that women are unaware of how unintentionally destructive they are. And when we're unaware, we don't try to get to the root of it. There were a few months where I went after gossip in my heart. I rooted it out. I sniffed it out. I dug it out. I felt so righteous. And this is a great crime, I see now. Not to chase our sin down to the corners of our souls, but to *achieve* the goodness of winning over it. This is a stark contrast to realizing (like a gift of sight) how much our debt was *before* we trusted God to clear us of it.

Our needs will escalate unless we realize what our "needs" are doing to the marriage. Likewise, his "sexual needs" are the outward façade of something deeper going on (namely, his unawareness of how big his debt is), and so are our needs for him to do, be, or say things correctly. It amazes me how women can speak out against porn, but men may not join their wives in the quest to sniff out critical spirits in the home. Or if they do, they learn quickly that it isn't exactly an adventure that strengthens the bond.

Consider the existence of romance novels and reality TV, and the draw they hold on women alone. Recently I read a fictionalized version of the Jacob/Leah/Rachel story from the Bible. Since the author is a Christian and the publishers were "Christian," I thought I was safe from this female-version-of-porn trap. But of course, I found myself counting the hours until the kids were down and my husband occupied so that I could pick it up again to see what will happen to these characters. The romance was clean but interesting, and the relationships were other-worldly. After all, what would it be like to have to share a charming husband with your sister? In truth, my husband is boring compared to these stories.

And of course, next to a porn star, I am boring as well. How can I blame him for comparing me to airbrushed images when I'm over here reading about other people's interactions to get a kick, however innocent? I really don't know how Christian writers can create stories that intrigue women and sleep soundly at night. Don't they know our greatest and worst sin is to think about (covet) something we don't have relationally? Do they believe we only sin when we think about (read about) the *sexual* parts of other people's relationships? No, it's a grave indulgence for a woman to think about the intimate relationships of others. This is a form of comparison, and it's no use calling yourself innocent because you're using stories from the Bible.

That's just as crazy as a man painting a picture of the story of Noah and his weird daughters-in-law for our men to look at late at night when they're bored. It wouldn't happen. Or if it did, we women would out it as evil—a distortion—right away. In the same vein, do yourself a favor and avoid the fictionalized stories of romances in the Bible. We have gotten into a weird thing, and it's high time some of the older women in the church responded with the ferocity of the spiritual mothers they are called to be. Someone somewhere must see the double standard and speak out. As a guy's desires escalate, so do ours.

4. It would explain a man's confusion when he witnesses the magnitude of his wife's pain upon revelation of the porn thing. Men are *constantly* bewildered as to how their wandering attentions could hurt us women so much. Have you noticed that? And can you flip the tables to see how baffled we are when they internalize our "help"

as criticism? We think, *What's his problem? I was merely showing him how I do it so that he can save himself some time. Now he's all shut down and angry with me.* To this day I wonder why my husband can't appreciate it when I recommend he wear his heavier coat on colder days. If God's suggestion to me were accurate, it would explain why the helpful winter coat proposal could actually *hurt* my husband.

It also explains his confusion at how much his sexual temptations hurt me. After all, men believe their mental sex lives have nothing to do with us. It's completely separate. Another topic entirely—not even related. And to see us crushed shows him just how big of a deal it really is. In the same way, I have put "home administration" in a box apart from my husband's ego. "Who cares how he receives my tone of voice," I've heard myself say. "The children need to be bathed, and the dog is barking at someone while supper burns on the stove. I need some help here." Before my disturbing lesson on the beltway, it would have completely baffled me to hear that everyday communications actually hurt my husband. Annoy him, sure, because he's selfish, but hurt him? *Preposterous*, I thought.

Now think about why our praise in public is more important to our men than the praise we dole out in private. Again, it would be good to put yourself in your husband's shoes in this instance, except with his sexual sin (or lack of) as the thing that could either kill you or give you life. Imagine you're in public and he's looking at a Victoria's Secret catalogue as you stand next to him. Would that not be more hurtful even than his doing it in private? I don't mean to be crass, but now consider your nagging in public. "Joe's not a handyman, he would *never* be able to fix our sink the way your husband did. You are so lucky." While the statement would hurt him both in private and

in public, the scenario where an audience could hear it would hurt your husband more and bring more shame upon yourself, of course.

No other thing can hurt a man in public like our criticism or negativity. As we've established, there are hundreds of books out there about a wife's criticism or negativity, but they're all soft. This message is wilder, still. It offers the possibility that even your help, your well-intentioned little tips and tricks which are of great worth to you, will shame him, especially if offered in public. Is it crazy to you that the simple statement *"Don't forget the diaper bag,"* can be hurtful to a husband? It was crazy to me at first, too. And it would be crazy to our men if we suggested that statement alone as the basis for huge hurt. Again, it's not a single statement that will send them over the edge. It's the hundreds of statements like that every day that spell disaster. Add them all up, and you're done before you had a chance.

If you bite your tongue against criticizing your husband, I'm really sorry about this, but think of that as his having a sexual fantasy in his mind without acting it out. I know it's probably awful to hear (especially if you're not open to these concepts, a camp into which most readers will likely fall), but Jesus said, "I tell you that anyone who looks at a woman lustfully has already committed adultery with her in his heart." Is it so much of a stretch to say that wishing your husband would do something different is the same as belittling him aloud?

I've learned to switch the roles and consider myself in his shoes with my criticism as his interest in porn. Anytime I'm confused, I try it out, and nine times out of ten, it's illuminating.

5. It would also explain why men don't talk about their pain from our words. Of course, men tend to use less verbiage in general, but also, it seems (even to them) absurd to be "hurt" when we remind them to do things around the house or offer helpful tips—especially when we're "*right*." Even if husbands acknowledged the hurt they feel from daily, common interactions with us, their own male rationale works against them here to further accuse them of being super-sensitive: a man's worst nightmare. Can you see your husband thinking "What the heck is wrong with me that her suggesting a different method ticks me off so much? What is my deal?!"

It sounds very much like our cry to God, "*What is wrong with me that his thought life would kill me?*" But from a man? Yeah, not so much. I don't know about yours, but my man's nature would not be so introspective organically. He may come to that conclusion with counseling or a support group, but he would have to be fighting his natural negative self-talk the whole time or, rather, the enemy's (and my?) talk.

In retrospect, I remember a few times where my husband tested the waters by complaining of my attitude in general. I went off on him, of course, naming all the pressures I have to face and tasks I don't get the luxury of choosing for myself, and he quieted right down. He has learned not to suggest anything without some form of push back, and that is unfortunate. I have a lot of work to undo. Since most men are in the same boat and have been convinced their desires are stupid, they don't bring it up anymore. After all, what's the point?

Instead, they buy more tools. Or watch more sports. Or play more video games, or stay at the office, whatever. These might not be an

"escape" for your husband in the way I'm explaining, but it's worth being open to that possibility because it might save a lot of heartache.

Imagine you're constantly a little hurt—chink, chink, chink out of your armor—after every encounter with your spouse. It's not enough to kill you, but after a few years of it, you crave an out. A straw will someday break the camel's back, unless the camel has supernatural powers. No wonder many guys think porn is no big deal—and honestly, it explains why they would compartmentalize and say it has *nothing to do* with their wives. Our counterpart to that would be saying that our reminding them to take their lunch would have *nothing to do* with how much we respect them. The truth is that some of our help serves to question their ability to handle things— like lunch. When someone says it like that, well then of course one has everything to do with the other.

So I can now understand why men tend toward modes of "escape" instead of connecting. Have you ever wondered what his deal is, why he tends to turn on the TV when a simple conversation could fix everything? At that very point, would it be such a stretch to think that a small "help" (even inadvertent criticism) from you could have been as damaging to him as his lust for other women is to your heart? If so, can you blame him for turning on the TV again? At least the TV has the façade of being safe.

If on occasion men tested the waters by saying "It's really painful when you say _____," there may be some hope. But when we respond by listing all the reasons we *had* to say that, it sends the message that we are above reproach and cannot do wrong.

Bottom line: men and women have conflicting definitions of "criticism."

6. It would explain a man's tendency to pursue other things, whether hobbies or work or social status. He never tries to change you because he knows firsthand how hurtful that would be. The "change" here applies even down to minute details like how we do things. I used to wonder why Joe never helped me the way I helped him. He never showed me a better way to wash the dishes. He would merely do them more efficiently. I caught him once, doing a household task in half the time it took me—and with a better tool. Why hadn't he ever told me of the more effective method? Any idea why? Is it possible he wouldn't want to be guilty of being judgmental since he's constantly on the receiving end of it and knows how hurtful it is? I asked him if this was indeed the case, and he said, "Of course." So instead, he escapes into a hobby. Obviously, many men have hobbies without the escapism aspect, but it's well known that a common tendency for dudes is to dodge the pressure by playing Call of Duty or World of Warcraft, and I believe this is why. If this seems unfair to you, it does to me at first glance, too. But here we are.

7. This also explains the level of shame that men feel in the sex area, which we do not feel. What if our version of their sexual sin tendency is truly our desire to change them, masked by our desire to "help" them? Would there be no higher shame on your head than to learn of your own motives if this were true? If Someone were to expose you, would you be able to even let the thought in as a possibility? Replay your own encounter with your husband as he left for work this morning. "Don't forget your wallet," we may say. Do they say the same to us? No. Why don't they? Because our mothering is hurtful, and they don't even *consider* inflicting the same on us. "But

the very last thing I meant to do was *hurt* the man by reminding him of his wallet," you say. "So I should be innocent!" And *again,* I agree with you. Yet God showed me this image of an armor with so many chinks in it that it looks like scrap metal. I don't think that because the damage was an accident that I am not responsible for it. Do you?

If I weren't this guilty (and exposed as such by God's merciful gift of repentance to me) then there would be no hope for our marriage because shame comes from the accusation that you're worse than another person. That means if my debts were smaller and if my friends are right when they say, "Go easy on yourself; you deserve to have a voice in your marriage," then they would be enabling the downward spiral. It's the same in my mind as my husband's guy friends saying, "You can look at other women as long as you don't touch," as though they're being exceptionally pious. Girlfriends, please stop telling me what I'm allowed to do in marriage and, instead, remind me of how much I've been forgiven for. Do not tell me to give myself a break, but remind me of the huge debt I once had, and I will do likewise for you. Then, ask your friends for the same favor. Repeat after me: "Girlfriends, please stop telling me what I'm allowed to do in marriage, and remind me of how much I've been forgiven." Ask this of your friends today.

Back to the concept that Joe thinks and does bad things: if he sees me as cleaner and more innocent than he, then shame reigns supreme, not grace. And if I agree and think that I'm human, sure, but I'm not *that* horrible, well then I heap on the shame whether or not I do it aloud or intentionally. And before we know it, we're on a downward spiral like a horrible ride that won't stop. That spiral isn't a steep one like the porn spiral but a slow, gradual one that

contributes to that phenomenon we always hear about: "We woke up one day, looked at each other, and said, 'Who *are* you?'" When I hear people say that, I disagree that they've drifted from one another, and I instead know that they've drifted from the reality of exactly how much God has absolved them.

I would even go so far as to say that shame is powerless unless there is a prideful person around. Let me tell you this funny little thing about shame that I've noticed. Joe's not ashamed of his sexual stuff with other guys in a room dedicated to the topic. But around me, his shame knows no bounds. That's because my pride speaks louder to him than my efforts of "taming my tongue." I could bite my tongue until it bleeds, but he still knows how I feel—repulsed. I'm trying hard to make this thing work, but the shame in him hears only the pride in me, and we're doomed each day before we even discuss what's for breakfast.

8. It would explain the constant suspicion our men think we wives feel when in fact we're not nagging them (or at least we don't think so). "Will you metro to work today or drive in and park?" Again, such a benign question, right? A man can take this as us suspecting them of doing something wrong. To us, it looks like an everyday question (and I still ask my husband this every few days). *But to them,* it looks like a trap for a "better answer" to be offered by us. Instant damage. If your spirit is yelling "BUT WAIT, THAT'S NOT FAIR!" right now, your spirit is right. It's *not* fair. It's not fair that we may be guilty of wounding our men 40 percent of the time in little well-intentioned reminders (like about remembering lunch), but that the other 60 percent of the time, they're suspecting

ill-intent when we have none. However, in truth, we're responsible for the entire 100 percent since *it was the 40 percent which caused the suspicion of the other innocent 60 percent.* You're right. It's not fair. Again, I agree with you. We will get to the definition of "fairness" later. But for now, ask your spirit whether it may have an ounce of truth. Warning: You may need to calm that spirit down before you ask. It's okay to be angry, annoyed, or even dismissive of this whole concept right now. But *forget my story, and forget this book.* Between your spirit and His, quiet down and ask whether these concepts are entirely ludicrous—or not.

This image of women's equal-and-opposite crime explains why we're always so danged suspicious and disappointed. I mean, maybe *you're* always happy with your man, but I'm not. Whenever I let my mind wander, I'm immediately tempted to wonder what the heck he is doing and why. This is also called judgment. The guy may be doing a great job at adulting, but I find receipts and wonder what the heck. Who knows where he is every Saturday while my peers and their families are doing bike rides with Dad in the lead. I watch the clock until he gets home, and when he does, his mind is somewhere else. He can't deal with us here at the house. We are in his way. And this is on his *good* days.

His very demeanor is hurtful. But if I remember *why* his demeanor is hurtful—namely, because I'm needy (Psalm 40:17), well then we have a new problem altogether. Being called needy by someone else is pretty insulting. But when you consider it to be a plausible reason for all the pain in your everyday interactions with your husband, being called "needy" has a freeing effect. If nothing else, it helps explain what's happening to me, and that's a step in the

right direction. In fact, I believe many of us are needy, and if culture would stop telling us how horrible a thing "needy" is, then perhaps we'd be able to move forward with what is under that layer and what a potential solution may be. I'm so tired of women discussing how they have needs their men cannot meet and how they *know* that God is the answer and they should just "rely on Him," but then the same women are surprised to hear that their *desire for positive change* in their men is what that neediness looks like. What else did you think it would look like? Why is this such a shock?

To me, when my husband leaves the toilet seat up and prefers his tablet over my company, the size of my disappointment indicates the size of the sin I am guilty of—wishing he were different. Usually, wifey self-help authors pause here with a disclaimer. "I'm not saying you're selfish for wishing your man would put the toilet seat down or spend more time with you," they croon. But that's *exactly* what I'm saying. And it's okay. Being a selfish person is common and even normal. It's you and it's me. Let's just get it out there. Admitting your selfishness may be a step toward healing.

If desiring positive change in our men (also called judging) were our main shared thing the way sexual sin is their main thing (the thing that all men understand), then no wonder we're consistently disappointed with them. Sometimes the bummers are small, and sometimes they're huge, but I'm constantly bummed out by my guy. Sure, we have fun many times, but then he pulls a jackass move, and I'm back where I started. Bummed. I'm not talking huge fights. I'm just talking daily frustrations that seem more common in me than in him. I realize now that this may be why all those wise old women on my wedding day seemed kind of sad. If magnifying my husband's

daily little faults is my greatest downfall, then of course I'd be disappointed in my man's hourly lameness.

Look at the flip side of this: just like when they look at porn, they're constantly disappointed by our wrinkles and flab. Try this experiment if I haven't given you a fear of hypothetical scenarios: think of the last time you were truly hurt or disappointed by your husband. If you're a typical wife (or even a stellar one), it won't be that long ago. Perhaps a few days. He was gruff. Or he didn't want to talk. Or he half-assed your anniversary with a *birthday* card on accident while your co-worker got six dozen roses and a couple's massage for *her* anniversary from *her* man. He was late coming home from work and didn't bother to call. He spent too much on something *he* wanted regardless of what's best for the family. He asked you to lose weight, or didn't defend you when someone said something untrue about you. He looked at porn again. He blew the grocery budget on booze or cigars. He bought a car and didn't tell you. I'm not asking you to conjure up his greatest offense, just the most recent thing that really bothered you.

Whatever it was, bring it to your mind. And since it's an imaginary exercise, remember, you're safe. You need not hold yourself to rectifying the mental image we're about to paint. But imagine with me that, like God suggested to me that day on the side of the road, that our "big misdeed" is our desire for our men to get better (or to change). In the same way their sexual sin hurts us, visualize our sin hurting them with the same magnitude, and see if this puzzle piece doesn't fit right in. *The size of your disappointment is the size of your self-righteousness.* What I mean is that a young wife could be crushed if her husband comes home from a business happy hour

drunk, while a more mature wife may simply sigh, roll her eyes, and get up early to make his coffee extra strong the next morning.

My point is that the young wife's sin is *not* her disappointment. It begins days before that when she's considering her station in life. Does her husband's goodness occupy her hope by default? Does she do her daily work trusting all the while that he'll do his, including the task of being faithful (or sober, or whatever)? If so, well then, sure, his drunken state would be painful indeed. Her hurt is not her sin; it's what she puts her assumptions in that is sinful. And if she trusted in him a lot, vehemently, then this display of weakness would be enormously tough on her. She was going to ask for a back rub, and he can't even put a sentence together. She had imagined (or trusted him for) so much more than this. I cannot go so far as to say that the older wife is "right" or genuinely "righteous," but it would seem she's onto something by everything I read in the Bible.

God has delivered when I've begged answers from Him in my pain. If 95 percent of men are tempted to fantasize and women have an equivalent counterpart—that is, the overwhelming tendency to their own version of disappointment, then it would explain our constant disenchantment.

9. It would explain our very nature. Only a crazy concept this extreme could explain how "the women's version" is not even a temptation at first. It's deeper than that. It actually is something that happens *before* I realize what's going on. And from what I gather, it's the same with young men. Before they realize what they're doing, sexual images and thoughts are there, but they're benign because they're just concepts, yet to be fed. The natural tendency is to feed them

(especially if they've been exposed to sold-out material), since the thoughts are already there, and who cares anyway, so these things get fed. Mouse clicks often come months or even years (sometimes decades) later. At first it's just a rabbit trail of thoughts, and correct me if I'm wrong, but young men can be surprised by where those trails end up, with a "wow," moment that accompanies a little shame.

With my logic, the same thing happens, but in the opposite direction. I realize an idea of mine is witty, and I admire it in the privacy of my mind. I enjoy the fact that I authored the idea all by myself. It really is benign at first. You teenagers and young twenty-somethings who may have gotten your hands on this book, beware of the silent self-admiration in your mind. The same thing may be developing in you—if you're anything like I am. I say beware because the rabbit trail in my mind resembles my male counterpart's, but instead of shame at the end, there's an element of pride, the opposite of my husband's brain. Can you see how the perfect storm is brewing? Shame on one side and pride on the other. What was meant to be flawless turned out to be horrid because someone (I) had a "good idea" and went with it.

What's worse is after a barrage of similar questions, I've seen my husband start to agree with me. I've seen his face change from "who cares, woman; get off my back about it" to "You're right, what's my deal; why do I hate orphans by default because I love buying flashy gadgets so much?" And these may have been my most disgraceful moments to date. When I see him agree with me, only then do I question what I've done with my attitude and words. I have made him feel inadequate, and there's nothing worse I could be doing for my marriage (or my family or the church or society) than that. This is not

something for me to keep an eye on or avoid; this is the perfect storm, and I've drowned long before I had a chance. It's way bigger than I am.

Another crazy thing that is stacked against us is the fact that there is this one weak spot in a man's armor, and it's the very shape and size of his wife's attitude. Other factors will shake a man around, but he'll beat them. A critical wife is the only thing that will penetrate that armor and finish off his resolve for good.

Here's a completely backwards story that, through this new lens, looks crystal clear and not backwards at all:

One day, my husband made the call to put a milk jug atop the fridge while he got something else. His hands were full, he needed somewhere to put the dumb jug, so up on the fridge it went. No one noticed that the milk jug was not completely atop the fridge. It had a few inches resting on top of the *door* of the freezer, so that the next person who opened the freezer door would have a jug come down on their heads. Well, the next person to open that door was Joe, so he had the fortune of bringing the jug falling down. But miraculously, and with insane reflexes, he caught the jug—not just clumsily, but by the handle, and looked up at me with that oh-my-gosh-did-you-see-that face. We exclaimed together and laughed at what a ninja he is.

A year later, we were in my mom's kitchen with my sister-in-law, grandmother, and preschool daughter. I tell you the people there because any man would recognize that these are the five women in the world who have something to say about how you're doing things if you're the dude-in-law there. There were four generations (plus a sister-in-law) worth of female voices in his ear: Get your daughter a drink; where's your phone charger? Have you lost weight? Did you

see the video I sent you? You smell like patchouli; how is your friend Russell? Can you help me reach that pitcher, please?

Hear me, women: To us, these are just ways to connect, but to him, it's a cacophony. A minefield. Why? I do not know, but the peppering of questions is like being covered in spiders to Joe. It's just a matter of time before he answers one question incorrectly, and all those voices turn on him and either cackle in shrilly unison or drill down on more questions. "What do you *mean* your job might not work out? I thought it was all set!" and his greatest fear is not having answers to them. Now, look. To me, not having answers to their questions is a good, safe thing. That's what they're there for.

I love going there with my hands in the air and telling them I'm at my wit's end. But not Joe. No, sir. We do not think alike. So anyway, that's the scene, and he's doing great handling it. "Russell's good; he'll be happy to hear you asked about him. He's enjoyed his time off work; here's your drink, little Ginny; here's that pitcher; it looks like it has some water spots on it though, so give me a sec to wipe it off; and I've only lost weight because you haven't been sending me your famous cookies, mother-in-law; I didn't like that job anyway and knew it could have been temporary, so thank God I have plans for this time between gigs and a good chunk of change saved up to keep your grandkids fed and clothed; and speaking of clothes did you see what the baby is wearing, by the way? I thought of you when I put that sweater on him; yeah, that video was funny; I love cats, too; and patchouli is cool since I don't smoke pot anymore; and Christ is my King." I'm telling you the man is a master with my family. There's truly nothing like it. He really charms the pants off us, and we have no idea how our words can (c)harm him in return.

Anyway, my story: as he's engaging them in their banter, he's drying wine glasses and because he does everything differently than the rest of the world, he puts the dry glasses on their side to dry. Of course, one of the stupid wine glasses (on its side) starts to roll off the counter, and no one sees it but me. I had a quick choice to make.

I didn't have enough time to run across the room and catch the glass myself because I was too far away. But I could have hollered across the room at Joe who was there, and who could have caught it with one hand. I did not. I stayed quiet, and watched the wine glass crash to the ground. "*Joe!!!*" the women all screamed. "Sorry," Joe said to them as he went for the broom and dustpan.

Now, you're either thinking I'm an idiot for not having screamed at him (early enough for him to catch the glass), or you think I'm a little proud of my composure. For a few weeks, I wrestled with that question myself, and finally, in the car, all three babies sleeping in back, I had a chance to ask him what would have made him feel more respected and manly in that case: my watching it crash, or my hollering and helping him to save the glass.

He answered that he felt more respected that I allowed the glass to crash down. This—still baffles me. What. The. Freak.

I told Joe that the milk jug incident flashed before my mind as I watched the wine glass start to roll, and I knew that it was worth the trashed glass for the one-in-a-million chance that something similar could happen in front of all my family—that perhaps he would have the miraculous reflexes to repeat such a stunt, and he would save the day—*without* a wife's across-the-room shout to "help."

When he heard that part, my reasoning behind not shouting, he lit up in a way I will never forget. His smile right then will always stick with me. I can never unsee his reaction.

Last night I asked Joe what he thinks women's "equal-and-opposite" sin or great temptation is that would be our version of men's shared thing. He said, "When women expect men to think like them, and we just don't. We won't. We can't."

10. And here's the most important thing: the hypothetical scenario of this temptation/sin (my assistance) being my version of my husband's lust problem would explain my main question. If you've forgotten it, reread the first two chapters. My main curiosity was how my husband's porn addiction could have devastated me instead of just setting me back a bit. For the first year and a half after I found this nasty yucko freak bull crap in my house, confusion reigned in my heart. Confusion reigned in my thoughts. Confusion reigned in my identity. Confusion reigned in my family, both nuclear and extended. Confusion reigned in my choices. I couldn't even decide what to eat for lunch some days because I was so confused. I had trusted the man so deeply, and it turned out he had a daily interaction (granted, mentally) with someone else. How then, could I trust a turkey sandwich to satisfy me more than salami? I was like a child, afraid of everything and knowing that every freaking sandwich was going to reneg on its promise to provide enjoyment or even sustenance. Now *that* is confusion: being depressed because everything you once trusted (down to your favorite deli meat) would now betray you. I was a head case. Confusion reigned. It ruled. It owned me.

If ever anyone close to you has died, then you know the confusion I'm talking about. It's almost more real than the actual pain.

I still prayed regularly, and I still heard God's kind voice in my ear, affirming His love for me. It is possible to be friends with God but not trust anything else on the planet anymore. It is possible to hear Him and yet still not know your arse from your elbow or which way is up—because of all the confusion. Confusion is not the same thing as doubt. I was confused. And the most confusing thing was "Why am I so hurt?" It did not make sense. Until, of course, God showed me this image.

I felt a wave of relief as I realized that this concept would explain the size of my hurt. How? I'll explain it, but I didn't know at first. Remember, I was still sitting on the side of the beltway as cars whizzed by. I remember getting a pen and paper out and writing madly all the things this suggestion would explain. It would explain so much. If God had exposed my mindset to be every bit as damaging to Joe as his lust was to *my* heart, then I suddenly had a lot of answers on my hands.

To get there, we have to be clear about something: I believe there's a third Party involved, obviously, since I've been talking about God and His influence a lot here. To oversimplify things, this is what I mean: there's a good God who loves everyone in a huge way. As in, we have no idea how to comprehend this love because it's so huge. And this God has a kind of problem on His hands because we're all busy hurting each other—sometimes accidentally, and sometimes purposefully. Whatever. Anyway, as you've seen, we cannot in our own power make things right. First of all, remember, when we say we're sorry, there's still a wound there. And second, we can't make things right in our own power because our power is just

not strong enough. No one on earth has the ability to make the stuff they've done completely right. So God decided to make the situation right for us by allowing His only Son to take the punishment that we all deserve for all of this colossal hurt that we're inflicting on each other. "Well, I never did anything that deserved *death*," you might say. "So that solution is a bit rash." Okay, well, good for you. But that's not really the truth. The truth is that we all deserve eternal separation from God for what we've done—and "eternal separation" is also known as the unending death known as hell.

The answer to why I was so hurt then is because I thought I was an innocent person, living in a hell on earth. Undeserved injustice. Receiving horrible treatment that I didn't merit.

Once I realized I deserved Joe's betrayal and more, the pain morphed into gratitude for the fact that I was not, indeed, getting what I truly deserve. No, I was getting a pretty sweet deal.

In the same way God opened my eyes to the magnitude of what I was doing (by "being good" and expecting Joe to do likewise), and the subsequent pain I was handing over to my spouse, He will reveal to you exactly what you've earned by just *living your life*. All you have to do is ask Him to show you. It will undo you completely. You may die from the revelation. It may be the end of you. But in that moment, if that same good God who loved you so much offered to pay the debt for you, and you accepted this gift with gratitude, then the very magnitude of your sin would be the new magnitude of your joy. And that's exactly what God offers. That's the "Jesus died for you" story. That's what all the Christians around the world are trying so hard to say.

When we accept Christ's sacrifice for us, we give up all of our rights. All of them. Even the right to voice our "harmless" opinions.

When God gave me just the shadow of an idea of what I am guilty of, well, then, suddenly the "rights" I'd clung to disappeared, including the right to be hurt. Does that *take away* my hurt? No, but it takes away my *right to be* hurt.

Here's how.

Beyond the Shadow of a Debt

Imagine you realize how hurtful you've been, and you'd now like to change. How will you do it? Sheer willpower? How do you see that working out for you? Envision it with me. You muster up the energy to be different, to be "perfect." What's your new tone? Authentic? Or forced?

Are you really doing anyone a favor by holding back those critical words and adding another point to your "righteousness account"? Do you applaud yourself quietly? Even today, I still sometimes bite my tongue and feel pious for "suffering so that the marriage doesn't deteriorate any." Don't stone me, but I suggest that this is the same as my husband's applauding himself for a good day if he only *looked* at porn, and lusted in spirit but did not act out his fantasy. Is this another crazy suggestion to you? If so, I can't blame you. I blame our culture of entitlement. And guess what: I bet 90 percent of men *do* applaud themselves for "mere" mental fantasies.

To be clear, forcing yourself to stop nagging is like treating a symptom instead of curing the disease.

Let's talk about fantasies for a minute, if you haven't already chucked this book in the fire, out the window, or God forbid, at your husband's face. My fantasy is the twenty-something version of my husband who, instead of fantasizing about who-knows-what,

helps me with the laundry and dishes. He doesn't just bathe the children; he's laughing with them while they splash. He earns enough money (and doesn't spend it) so that we can take a trip as a family to fun places each year, and then he whisks me off alone every once in a while for our own little adventure. Of course, he's made arrangements for trusted childcare beforehand, including food and special crafts/activities for the children so the babysitter is charmed and not too burdened by their whining while we're in paradise. The babysitter is overcompensated, so I don't feel the need to repay her more than what he's arranged.

Since that's unrealistic, let's take it down a level. Let's explore a more reasonable fantasy of mine: On regular days, what if he (in my mind) comes home from the workday and asks me engaging questions that remind me he's been thinking about me, such as "How did the grocery store trip go, Meg, considering you had three children under four years old with you? How did you make it happen? I bet it was your amazing creativity at work." This is my fantasy. And I don't believe it's so far out of reach that someone somewhere doesn't have a husband like that. He may exist somewhere.

But hey you know what? I figure I'll take what I can get. When dude comes home, he's tired, so I don't get on him when he doesn't help with the dishes or constant crumbfest on the floor. Instead, I just ask him whether he paid the vehicles' insurance, and why he was late, no big deal. Meanwhile, he wonders quietly why I'm such a fretful witch for nagging about it. And we have ourselves a downward spiral. We're both a mess and believing we each deserve a notch better than what we've got. Not a fantasy—just a notch.

By taking *what I can get* out of my husband, I'm not doing him—
or myself—any favors at all.

Reinforcements to Our Self-Righteousness

Recently I heard a sermon series on men and women, including
their differences, their purpose, and their potential pitfalls. Seventy
percent of it was directed toward men. When the preacher finally
turned to how women can improve, there were a bunch of jabs at
men thrown in. It was awful, and it was the common approach
for today's congregations. But I want to point out an odd thing
I noticed: in the section geared toward men, the preacher (young
hip guy, you know the type) said a bunch of stuff we've all heard
before. No one was surprised to hear his observations, that if a man
sins, it's either because he's acting aggressive (porn, anger, selfish
ambition) or being passive (more porn, laziness, refusal to engage,
absenteeism).

But when the women's part came up, he said, "Now let's talk
about you ladies." You could have heard a pin drop. And I was right
there with his congregation—I was on the edge of my seat. *What's
he going to tell us?* No one knew. It struck me how every sermon
about women's stuff is interesting because it's all novel. It's all fasci-
nating because the preacher has to (at least partially) come up with
something since women have built up a façade of being righteous.
Dude can't simply repeat what he knows women can do with their
tongues and mindsets. The world simply won't have the age-old
truth because it's been said before with very little impact. That
preacher, by the way, did his best, but he has no idea what women
need to hear. Only the kind, gracious Holy Spirit does.

Everyone knows aggression and passivity are men's Achilles heel. But women's is news to all. Interesting and fresh info here. *What's the pastor going to say?* Gossip? Sure, but gossip next to porn is pretty yawn-worthy, and pastors act like one has the power to destroy entire societies while the other gets a short mention in each sermon. No, self-righteousness is, by nature, impossible to see in oneself, and women want to hear every sermon except the self-righteousness one. In fact, women *can't* hear it. We're deaf to it. Again, that's the very nature of self-righteousness. It's the only true *disability*.

This explains why we don't see the same treatment of men's sins versus women's, and also why women flit from one study to the next without grieving the fact that they may be holding back God's very bride—the church—by the way they think about and talk to their husbands.

When a preacher addresses the wives in his congregation, I'm always disappointed to hear a bunch of jokes thrown in while the same preacher yells at men during *their* part. Is it possible he (in his mind) must approach preaching this way because he's been convinced we wives tend to be "holier" or at least more well-intentioned than men? If so, then God help us.

And that's just the men-versus-women sermons. There are so many messages which address the men's stuff (selfish ambition, anger, greed, malice, dishonesty, lust), while women sit back and nod, saying, "It's good he's listening to this." Or, "If he would just come to church, the preacher would tell him how to live right by me and everyone else."

Don't misunderstand: women are willing to admit that they are just as sinful as men. However, I have yet to see women point out

where exactly their sins compare and show them *just as* damaging as men's sins. I also have yet to see women treat their own sins quite as harshly as they do their male counterparts'. I don't see women attending accountability groups for their share of the damage the way I do see men flocking to them, sometimes at their wives' nudging. Sure, there is the occasional one or two women trying to get out of a particular addiction, but usually they don't identify their addiction as their constant need for their men to change. If women took their own words seriously and if women dug deep to find out their *grievous* sin, the one that does *just as much* damage as men's lust, then we would see things like the volume of books/programs/ discussions match or exceed those we find in the "men's sins" area.

But we don't. We see books for women which are meant to *encourage* them. May I suggest women need less encouragement and more reality? It's not encouraging to realize you're guilty of as much hurt as your husband. But I can tell you firsthand: *it is true freedom.* You can be forgiven of a debt that otherwise would have had you and your family in eternal slavery. If you need encouragement beyond that, then you don't realize the size of that debt you've been cleared of—or what true eternal slavery looks like.

We've been blinded, somehow, somewhere along the way. It probably happened early on, at the point when we heard good logic coming from our own mouths and silently congratulated ourselves for the cleverness. For me anyway, it was in the early years of my marriage when what I vocalized actually *worked* (temporarily) to make my husband shape up. He had nothing on my wit. It was a powerful feeling, and Satan must have loved watching me relish it. The very thing that Joe liked in me first (besides my butt) was my

ability to say things in a way he hadn't heard before—in a way that made him think. He liked using his brain, and so it was an attractive mental exercise to hang out with me. But then, when we got married, of course my conversational acumen started working against him in little ways. Ways we could both agree were helpful at first. The same good wit and logic worked to conceal haughty tones or patronizing remarks. We were done before we ever had a chance to begin. And the worst part is that I thought things were going great.

Earlier I touched upon the suspicion that my husband sometimes has when I've genuinely done nothing wrong. Despite what I've made you think, there are times I don't use my cleverness against him. I'm pretty much the worst wife in the world (thank Goodness, I've learned), but sometimes I'm just asking whether the dog's been fed or not. In these instances, my husband wants to interpret my tone, but he has this database of past experiences to draw from, and that database has some hurtful crap. For the last eight years, I've done what I thought was right and unwittingly taught him to distrust my words and attitudes. Now this occasional innocence is a casualty of war, a real tragedy. I truly just need to know whether I'm about to overfeed the dog, and this is one household task of about a hundred that we need to collaborate on every day. But when you contaminate the water, the whole supply is infected. Cry all you want, and I'm with you. It sucks. This realization was particularly painful because now I need forgiveness for doing *right*.

Believe it or not, you *do* need forgiveness for all the right you've done. Have you ever heard the term "filthy rags?" We toss around scripture that says no one is righteous, but then we're shocked when someone says that our good deeds are horse crap. It's a wild thought,

but Jesus did go to the cross for both my bad days and the days I didn't hurt anyone, the days I yelled at my husband as well as the days I was his joy and crown. Total depravity means my very existence needs forgiveness because my definition of "good" will never be spot on. And yours does, too. But instead of freaking out about that and calling me a weirdo, rejoice with me in the fact that that forgiveness has already been given. The rest is just helpful for perspective. For me, it adds to my gratitude.

Consider this account from Sharon Drury:

> Suzanne sat in her regular place last Sunday as Pastor Mike preached a powerful holiness message, calling his congregation to commit their all to Christ. He challenged the attendees to enter the sanctified life of service to others, putting off all concern for self. He especially emphasized overcoming ugly besetting sins such as lust, anger, pornography, hunger for power, and pride. Suzanne listened attentively and mentally examined her own life as he listed the sins: Nope, nope, nope, nope, and nope. She wasn't a proud woman, she just was being honest: none of these sins were her problems—and she could honestly say she was free of sin—at least these sins. However, her mind wandered to thinking about her husband and some of the Christian men she worked with and she found herself thinking of them. Yep, yep, yep, yep, and yep—men really need this cleansing from God.

Suzanne is sinning, but not the way Pastor Mike keeps mentioning.

Drury goes on to say:

> A call to surrender self and serve others, for many women, is to call them to do the very thing they are already doing and perhaps have done too much. Some women have so negated themselves and merged their lives into others that they hardly have a self. Many women have such low self-esteem that their self is nowhere available to surrender.

And finally, she mentions that pastors have the tricky task of preaching to such women: "Males preach total self-abdication as the goal of consecration, while for many women it may be their major temptation—pouring out their lives for others *instead of for God.*" This pouring out seems so sacrificial, but now we know better.

The Spiral Up

Another way to put it is that grace cannot exist without sin. If you see a deeply happy marriage, it's not because the people therein are particularly submissive or faithful to one another. Sorry. You're looking at something else. If it's a truly contented relationship, then it's because of grace. And again, if there's grace, that's because there was and is sin. It's not because things have always been tidy.

If nothing else, please hear this: shame is powerless without a proud person around. It dissipates like mist. And grace cannot exist

where there was not first failure, disappointment, and hurt. Betrayal is a canvas for art of the most beautiful kind.

Here's another scenario where pride and shame go hand-in-hand to keep everyone disconnected from God and one another. Perhaps if you see it in this tour of a certain downtown Chicago neighborhood, then you can nix it from your own home.

There's this woman in Chicago who saw an odd dynamic between affluent suburbanites and uptown residents. We'll call her Sher, because hey, that's her real name. Sher wanted to address this dynamic she saw, but it wasn't as easy as she had first thought. First she visited the poor in their neighborhoods. Then she started eating with them at soup kitchens (resisting the general tendency of suburbanites to ladle the soup). Next, she rented out a crack house in their neighborhood and moved in. She's been there for eight years now. People paid more and more attention as her thing grew interest. Her purpose in this old crack house was not to come "save the day," but to just *be* with these ignored people and then be with them some more. I visited her house a few years ago, and what I learned there stuck with me. Believe it or not, it changed my perspective of porn and hurt in marriage.

The affluent people who visit Sher have *no choice* but to think long and hard about their own role in this same neighborhood (and their distant neighborhoods, too). Most suburbanites take one of two paths when they see what Sher is doing: They either donate their time, energy, and money to her, or they write her words off as judgmental against rich people. I actually did both and still feel the temptation to do both. It's my first reaction whenever she speaks— even about her plans for the day. I'm tempted either to donate, serve,

or roll my eyes at her Robin Hood philosophy. Do you know what that is? That's pride and self-righteousness in me, and in my suburbanite friends. And guess what: her downtrodden neighbors in the shelters and on the streets don't get the luxury of serving or rolling their eyes. They're exposed, and waffle between shamed and shameless.

You see, suffering does this thing where you're suddenly exposed. Sher's neighbors are suffering, and they're exposed. The buttoned-up people who come to visit make themselves vulnerable, too, but on their (our) terms, and they (we) maintain the ability to go back to our secluded homes when we're tired, bored, or afraid of the poor. My favorite part about Sher is that, when talking about this escapism, she says that's okay. The only thing that's not okay is to maintain your *power* as you go home, and that's where many people lose her.

There's gunfire daily (sometimes hourly), addiction, sex in the street, and pooping on sidewalks. Their stuff hangs out, and they know it, and who cares. But we who are well rested and know where our next meal will come from—we have a power to cover up at our discretion. When we think it's best, we can monitor our words or behavior. Sher's neighbors cannot. They actually have more pressing matters to consider than how they appear to others. We are a little more put together, and I'm not saying that's evil. I'm saying it's a natural mask for evil. It's the perfect environment for mold, if you will. It is something you cannot see growing unless someone rips the cover off and shines a light in there.

Sher has stayed in this unique neighborhood for years partly because she wants to communicate to herself, others, and to God

that she recognizes she's no different than anyone. And to be clear, suburbanites aren't the enemy; it's the power that they often maintain that's the opposing force.

Still confused? Okay, put it this way: When I resolve to "watch my mouth" with my husband (without seeing how damaging my outlook/attitude is), I am in effect, ladling soup "for the poor," and enjoying the feeling it gives me. I'm doing them some kind of "favor" by "sacrificing" for the greater good or for the other person who is exposed and out there, not as capable of containing *their* mess. The whole exercise actually puts another layer of epoxy over my mold so that it can continue to grow, making everyone sick. We can all go home and keep the system of pride and shame in place, never upsetting what we've worked so hard to establish. Instead of serving them, I've further sealed their fate. If I bite my tongue as a favor to my husband but harbor that criticism in my heart (like I often do), I've not done us a service but quite the opposite: I've exercised my power, further cementing our unhealthy relationship of pride and shame. And I have no business doing that.

If you'll remember, I said that suburbanites see Sher's example and do one of two things: They either donate their time, energy, or money (the equivalent "favor" a wife does when she piously watches her words instead of begging God for a glimpse of her erased debt); or they write off her Robin Hood approach and say, "There's no sin in being rich." If the pride of a betrayed wife is similar in nature to the pride of a semi-comfortable middle-class person, then there's a parallel to their dismissal method, too. And that brings me to the wives who dismiss their freaky sicko husbands as—freaky sickos. The root of pride grows stronger with every dismissal.

Should you move to the slums? Don't be silly. I'm not the one to tell you that. Instead, take that "condition" you see as him (or them) having that "disease," and apply it to your hypothetical self in your clean home and clean, pious heart. Then, consider "moving in" with your husband in his unpredictable neighborhood. The relocation can save you from your own power. And now we're talking about potential for grace in a marriage. Sher calls it restoration.

"Power?" Yes. Being offended, while understandable in many cases, gives a false sense of power. In fact, before there's even a "betrayal," I see (from decades of hearing sermons and reading Christian books) that wives have been handed a certain power they aren't meant to handle. As male preachers beat the pulpit against sexual temptations in the church (with the occasional side note for women to watch their mouths at home, so they don't contribute to the problem), we're given a certain "all clear" which we should not have. In the same way money gives families the choice to isolate themselves from certain pain (that is, move away from the ghetto), this spiritual "proceed with caution" message has given women a power to hunt down *other* problems in our lives so that we needn't get to the root of what's really happening. Are suburbs the enemy? That's laughable. It's like saying a wife's commitment to memorizing scripture is wrong. And conclusions like those are another indication some people will do anything they can to avoid the true point: we suburbanites and wives *deserve* hell, and anything other than that judgment should be reason to party. So no, the 'burbs are not bad, and neither are spiritual disciplines. What's bad is the sense of superiority that comes with those things before we're even aware of it. Once you feel superior, the game is over. There's not much hope

left for your marriage or your community. The rifts we see now will become lines, then divisions, and eventually ruptures.

The sneakiest part of this is that the outward appearance of both choices are pretty similar. That is to say, loving on others can be done because you can't help yourself, or it can be done because you're forcing yourself. For some people, memorizing scripture is a simple byproduct of their excitement for this new freedom. For others though, memorizing scripture and serving at the soup kitchen can just be the "right thing to do," thus subconsciously adding to the debts that others owe them. It is not that those working for that wonky motive would recognize what's happening. They won't. It's impossible because *once perspective changes, so does motive.*

I talked with Sher recently about the change in my heart, and how that terrible suffering of betrayal was the best thing that ever happened to me, by far. She said, "You know, Meg, this concept we're given from birth that sin separates us from God? Yeah, I completely disagree with that—nothing drives us to Him like the exposure of our wrongness." She's saying she knows how I could have felt relief—not shame—when I finally got a glimpse of the size of my sin.

No Debt About It

B efore I go on, we need to take a minute and explain what God did *not* say to me and thus, what I am *not* saying to you.

I'm not saying you caused your own hurt. I'm not saying you brought this particular consequence on yourself. I'm not saying the pain you feel is the direct result of what you did. Although it may be. That's not my story to tell. My point is God only showed me what I deserve, not what I *caused*.

I'm also not saying that you caused *his* sin. No one can cause another person to sin. Your critical spirit can *hurt* him, but it cannot make him do anything wrong. Likewise, he can't make you nag, although it might feel like he can. He can discourage you and reject you and even abuse you, but that does not cause you to sin. Your own nature does that for you (insert huge sarcastic high-five for that one).

I'm also *not* saying you're responsible for your husband's mental escape or his horrible sloth regarding housework. You're not burdened with the job of fixing him or yourself. You did not cause his sin. Neither is it your job to clean it up.

I'm not saying he's a good dad. He might be the worst, who knows. He also might be cheating on you right now. The truth is that his

behavior is none of your fault. He might owe you a lot. He may never be able to repay the debt he's incurred by damaging you or his family.

I'm also not saying your hurt is a mirage or fabrication. Believe me, there's no torture quite like this betrayal. When a husband fails, life can seem like it's not worth the effort. No one gets it more than I do, which again made me wonder—why am I so done in by this? I could spend a whole book on the description of this searing pain. In fact, I might. I'll never say porn doesn't hurt wives. And I'll never say that that hurt is bogus or unsubstantiated. If there's a lump in your throat as you read this part because of the simple, sheer, incredibly terrible hurt, please read on because there's a sweet hope on its way.

You and I were both born into a race that's doomed because of the first, original fall of mankind. One dude—the first one ever—sinned against God, and you and I are now in that dude's cursed family, ill-fated to self-destruction.

You see, hurt turns into sin before we know it. His neglect or abuse can hurt you, and that is not in your control. Those wounds are genuine, and you can feel free to set this book down and weep at any point because that wound is real. And it's huge. And it deserves the same deep grief that you see at funerals. But when you're ready, steel your heart for what's next: the temptation to go from hurt to resentful is usually imperceptible. You cross the line before you know it. At least, if you're anything like I am, you're resentful before you realize it. It's a blurry, shifty line, and that's not fair, is it? It's not fair, unless you consider it a good thing to sin before realizing it (which incidentally, I do and will explain why in a bit).

Before resentment settles in, though, when you're still confused, those tears are a canvas for God's beautiful artwork. I'll show you

what I mean. But first, I need to warn you: This gets really weird. It's going to be hard, and in the next few pages you're going to wonder where I'm going with this. But it's what He gave me, and it may be what He wants to give you, too.

So what am *I saying?* I'm saying that if you've been bombarded for years by our culture telling you that you "deserve" better, you "deserve" a break, you're "good enough just the way you are," you "deserve the best," you're "worth it," well, guess what, you don't, you don't, you're not, you don't, and you're not.

Sorry.

I wish I hadn't been raised and immersed in that coddling culture, but I had been, and it was not fun to be yanked out of it. And when I was given the Truth, it was eye-opening because at the time I didn't think it was so wild to think *I deserved fidelity.*

Here's the truth about what I deserve: On my own, I deserve complete and forever separation from God as well as total and unending separation from everything good and enjoyable in my life. And, scandal of scandals, so do you.

No wonder this story will seem like a rant to most wives so far—many have never had a whiff of what they truly deserve. I say this with all joy, too, because I know that what I deserve on my own is not the end of my story. We'll get to that in a minute. For now, I do want to emphasize that of all the things I'm not saying, I most certainly *am* saying I deserve hell for my worldview in early marriage (among other ongoing things).

Both can be true. You *can* refuse to be abused while you acknowledge you deserve it. I deserve Joe to cheat on me, but I won't stick around while he does. Get comfortable having what you *deserve* in

the same room with *what you won't put up with.* I won't put up with abuse, although I see now that I have earned it.

Here's what I mean by that.

Just a minute ago I was telling you how it felt when I found his sin. I said, "When a husband fails, life can seem like it's not worth the effort," and I imagine a lot of hurting readers agree with that feeling. It feels like hell on earth.

The purpose of this story is to illustrate how this same statement would sound coming from a husband's mouth: "When my wife is unkind, life can seem like it's not worth the effort." If your heart doesn't soften at the thought of that magnitude of discouragement coming from a man, then consider your heart one huge block of ice. And through the next few pages, hopefully you'll begin to thaw out a little bit.

I'm telling you what God told me after I'd been tortured and tormented for eighteen months by my husband's multiple lives. Since I'm obviously not an orator or marriage expert, I went to the Bible to explain it for me. And this was frustrating because the Bible talks about sexual immorality all day, but kind of leaves out the wife's equivalent (of betrayal by words and attitude). Sure, there's a proverb or two about the annoying wife, but the whole Book is jammed packed with rules about sex. So men have plenty of material here, and women like me are left feeling mighty clean and superior.

To make matters worse, the Bible (and its preachers) are constantly harping on self-sacrifice, and when you consider how many floors we sweep, butts we wipe, dishes we wash, and mouths we feed, it's kind of natural to feel we're hitting a home run in the

self-sacrifice area. Especially when our entire culture coddles us—coddles both our sin *and* our goodness.

So the Bible kind of seemed to go against my generous God's suggestion to me in the car that day. At least, *most* of what I'd been taught from the Bible did. And then I found this – the greatest Speaker who ever lived just happened to put a story into His teaching for me:

The Parable of the Unmerciful Servant

²¹ Then Peter came to Jesus and asked, "Lord, how many times shall I forgive my brother or sister who sins against me? Up to seven times?"

²² Jesus answered, "I tell you, not seven times, but seventy-seven times.

²³ "Therefore, the kingdom of heaven is like a king who wanted to settle accounts with his servants. ²⁴ As he began the settlement, a man who owed him ten thousand bags of gold was brought to him. ²⁵ Since he was not able to pay, the master ordered that he and his wife and his children and all that he had be sold to repay the debt.

²⁶ "At this the servant fell on his knees before him. 'Be patient with me,' he begged, 'and I will pay back

everything.' [27] The servant's master took pity on him, canceled the debt and let him go.

[28] "But when that servant went out, he found one of his fellow servants who owed him a hundred silver coins. He grabbed him and began to choke him. 'Pay back what you owe me!' he demanded.

[29] "His fellow servant fell to his knees and begged him, 'Be patient with me, and I will pay it back.'

[30] "But he refused. Instead, he went off and had the man thrown into prison until he could pay the debt. [31] When the other servants saw what had happened, they were outraged and went and told their master everything that had happened.

[32] "Then the master called the servant in. 'You wicked servant,' he said, 'I canceled all that debt of yours because you begged me to. [33] Shouldn't you have had mercy on your fellow servant just as I had on you?' [34] In anger his master handed him over to the jailers to be tortured, until he should pay back all he owed.

[35] "This is how my heavenly Father will treat each of you unless you forgive your brother or sister from your heart." Matthew 18:21–35

We began this chapter to disclaim what I'm *not* saying. So, in light of scripture, here's what I *am* saying: I believe I was allowed to be tortured until I realized how much I had been cleared of. And if you feel like this thing is torturing you, it may not be an illusion. He may be allowing that for you.

It's possible for my husband to be just as hurt as I am because of my constant assumption that he thinks like I do (and therefore should do as I do). If that's the case, Jesus is calling my guy's sins "a hundred silver coins." Chump change. To me, they should be forgiven quickly and even easily.

The only problem with me when I read this parable is that I look around in my life, consider the offenses others have done to me, and piously close my eyes, raise my chin, and say that I forgive them, even though it's "so hard." Then I hand Joe his lunch on the way out the door and snap at him not to spend money at a drive-through like he did yesterday. And I call that "collaboration." Not nagging. Not sin. Do you see what I'm getting at? I look around for all those debts God showed me in this parable because I want to settle up and not head to jail. I want to be debt free.

But, hours later, in telling my husband how to do stuff, I'm telling him he owes me two here, ten there, and a fiver each day, if he knows what's good for him. Instead of making me more merciful, my interpretation of that parable has made me more pious, more self-righteous than ever.

Here's another way to explain the same notion: Recently, the preacher at our church delivered a sermon about forgiveness and how forgiving your brother is an act of obedience. The dude's up there giving it his all, and at the apex of his message, he said, "You

know what the most powerful sentence in the world is?" And of course, this desperate crowd was on the edge of its seat because who the heck doesn't have anyone to forgive? The congregation held its collective breath as Rev paused dramatically. "*I forgive you,*" he said with pageantry.

I could have died. He missed the point of forgiveness completely!

Here's the truth: it's better to be on the *other side* of the forgiving equation. It's more liberating, more powerful, more exciting, more clarifying, more energizing, more *everything* to say, "I'm so sorry." Believe me, I've been on both sides.

The instant God showed me the picture of my husband's dented, injured heart that day in my car, I switched sides from being the wounded to being the baddie—in a big way. Instantly, as I described before, a flood of conviction—and relief—swept over me. To this day, I'll always seek, knock, and ask to be on the side of "I'm so sorry," instead of "I forgive you." The act of obedience thing is all but gone when you see how much of your debt has been paid because it's only logical (not even very emotional anymore) to forgive your fellow servant of a little coinage when you were just cleared of a million bucks.

Trust in Marriage

I've heard my whole life that trust is the foundation of marriage. "You can't have a marriage without trust." Well hey, I disagree. I don't believe women should work on trusting their husbands, although, that would be easiest for us. It would be a feel-good exercise to "build trust." And it would be so comforting to achieve it—to be able to trust our men. I feel cozy just thinking about it.

But I believe we need to trust forgiveness through the Forgiver, not our husbands. Here's what I mean:

The apostle Paul wrote letters to some churches, his friends, who were suffering political and economic injustice. But instead of praying for the government to change and instead of praying for financial provision, look what Paul prayed for on behalf of these hurting people in Ephesians 3:14–21:

> For this reason I kneel before the Father, from whom every family in heaven and on earth derives its name. I pray that out of his glorious riches he may strengthen you with power through his Spirit in your inner being, so that Christ may dwell in your hearts through faith. And I pray that you, being rooted and established in love, may have power, together with all the Lord's holy people, to grasp how wide and long and high and deep is the love of Christ, and to know this love that surpasses knowledge—that you may be filled to the measure of all the fullness of God. Now to him who is able to do immeasurably more than all we ask or imagine, according to his power that is at work within us, to him be glory in the church and in Christ Jesus throughout all generations, for ever and ever! Amen.

Receiving forgiveness is better than receiving comfort.

So in Bible study or home group or house church or whatever the hipsters want to call it, when it's time to go around the circle for prayer requests, consider praying for something way wilder than health for someone's Aunt Dorothy or that their husbands' business ventures take off, or even that their cancer will be healed. In light of the Spirit's power, which is what you *could* ask for them, what is the rest?

If the apostle Paul joined our prayer meeting today, he would probably dismiss our circumstantial troubles now as he did then. Was Paul heartless? Or had he realized something the rest of us still completely miss?

In the same way, I won't beg for Joe to be faithful anymore, although I do mention it in prayer. Instead, I pray most fervently for power from the Spirit, which will root me and establish me in love, no matter what the guy is up to as we speak. And if I tell you that I'm praying for you (and I am), know that I will not pray for your circumstances to change but for your heart to change and for your spirit to receive whatever sweet message God has for you in the middle of your pain. Because that's so much better than a change in circumstances.

So no, marriage is not based on trust of the other person. It's based on trust of forgiveness, and the ultimate Forgiver.

For some reason, God showed me these images, and now the cancelling of debts is what gives me joy today, not hoping Joe is faithful to me. Mainly because he's *not* faithful (in the way I thought he was) and also because the poor dude crumbles under that kind of pressure. Trust is a tricky thing. I wonder whether the trust we put in our husbands is perceived as pressure to be good. Or moral.

Or caring. Or on time. Or sober. Or dressed properly, or whatever else comes out of our mouths today.

I believe human nature and our enemy have both gotten hold of our hearts in this area, and now assign the word *trust* to mere expectations and assumptions in our hearts. I expected Joe to be faithful, and he was not. Most women and counselors would say I *trusted* him. Call me jaded, *or call me free,* but I will never "trust" Joe with those expectations again. I can *hope* for fidelity, but I won't expect him to be faithful. If he's faithful to me, it's an undeserved gift I am now thankful for, not something I have the right to demand.

The man has two tablets, two smart phones, two laptops, and our home PC. If I were to trust that he didn't look at porn on any of them today, I'd be misguided, not because he's a creep, but because I've been given an assignment that should have me busy enough: that of rooting out my own tendencies and thanking God for paying the debt I incur for them. Even if Joe's innocent of it all, and I *trusted* him today, I would drive myself crazy making sure that trust is secure. I see now that that version of trust is a flimsy, suspicious thing and has no business in my side of the marriage. Especially if *trust* is really *pressure* in disguise.

If God were to give me His definition of "trust," then perhaps I'd agree that trust is the foundation of marriage. But until that day, I won't rely on this world's (or the Church's) version of "trust." I stand only upon the images He did give me, and they're of my putting pressure on Joe and calling it "trust."

So I focus on what God has shown me about my sin, my temptations, and my tendencies, which I have explained as best I can here. I focus on them with the same intensity I focused on Joe's fidelity in

those early days after the "reveal." Those days, I *needed* his sin to be rooted out. Today, though, I work on rooting out my own sin with the same crazy intensity.

And it's beautiful. Imagine this: a wife who's been cheated on understandably goes around her house, looking for clues. Today, I do the same thing, but I'm looking for clues of my superior, self-righteous attitude because it'll kill our marriage if I don't. Porn stars are no threat to our marriage compared to my expectations, assumptions, and self-righteousness.

He Left No Room for Debt

Recently, I heard from a tired-looking woman whose husband had cheated. Their marriage was over. I had met her at a seminar that focused on forgiveness. We had just spent hours going over how to forgive someone, why to forgive someone, and what it actually looks like. At one point we had "table talk" discussion time, where we go around the circle and everyone tells of a time they put forgiveness (or saw someone else putting forgiveness) into action.

The tired lady spoke up and said that after her husband cheated, she was devastated. Heartbroken. I cried as she described her hurt. There really is nothing quite as hurtful to a wife as marital betrayal. She went on to say that after a few years, she mustered up the grace and energy and chutzpah to do the *right thing*. It took everything in her, and she said the Lord sustained her as she did it. She marched up to her ex-husband's front door and knocked. When he answered, she did the most difficult thing she's ever done (or even imagined) in her life: She said, "I forgive you."

The other women clucked their tongues and nodded in affirmation, and I don't doubt her (or their) sincerity. They all obviously believed that that act was brave, sacrificial, and the perfect picture of humility. However, I couldn't shake the feeling that something here

was very wrong. "I forgive you," while a good start, always seems so self-righteous. And I'm starting to realize *it is self-righteous.* Not to mention, sad old tired-eyes looked tormented by her hurt. She was *still* in obvious pain. I mean, she was haggard.

The leader of that seminar, Monica Gill, on the other hand, told a similar story with a drastically different ending. She explained how when something goes wrong in a relationship, whether intentionally or not, a debt is incurred. She used the example of the very hurtful relationship she had had with her father. When her father was horrible to her, it needed to be made right. But her dad was not changing, let alone reversing course and asking what to do to make it right. No, he was continuing to abuse her, even as she grew, married, and started a family of her own.

Monica lived in a state of perpetual forgiveness of her father. She always forgave him quickly and completely, even when it hurt. And it did hurt because the abuse just kept coming. And despite what we're told (how forgiveness "feels so good" and you feel "a weight off your chest"), her constantly forgiving him didn't seem to heal her heart or give her hope.

Then one day God gently showed her that no one was paying the debts this guy was incurring by being a jerk. God quietly showed her the option to pay the man's debt if she wanted to.

Monica, in what I believe is *true* heroism and *true* humility and *true* sacrifice, spent time identifying all the things *she had done wrong* in her relationship with her father. She rooted out the ugly, nasty things she'd done, including things that some people would have called mere boundaries or self-preservation. She dug up her attitudes of defensiveness and indignation (which in anyone else's

eyes would have been justified), and she laid them on the altar of the Almighty God.

He, with infinite kindness, showered her with His approval, and she made the same trek to the perpetrator's house that the tired-looking lady made. But Monica, instead of saying, "Dad, I forgive you," said "Dad, I'm so sorry for everything I've done to mess up our relationship."

Her description of what this felt like was moving. She said it didn't feel like forgiveness, it actually felt like she was dying. She said it felt like she was cutting herself. Because it's hard to cancel your dad's debt when he's done this, but it's straight-up *death* to tell a perpetrator of *the things you did and attitudes you maintained* to incur a debt in that relationship.

Monica doesn't look like she's suffering. She exudes joy and peace. She enjoys life. She's not tired-looking at all. She acts young and vibrant, even as life throws her curveballs. She's grounded, and she's well. She seems whole. Does she still struggle with the things life deals us as women? Oh, you betcha. She's not immune to past, present, or future hurts. But her relationship with her dad is clean and right because of *her* payment. Her heart is wide open to everyone. She loves people so passionately that it's refreshing just watching her operate in daily life. Her joy would be enviable if it weren't so contagious.

Now, we've waded into some pretty heady waters here, but there's one final question I had, and it starts with the revealed truth that I deserve hell. And marital infidelity is hell. Does this mean I deserve a cheating husband? Yes. Unquestionably.

This, however, is hard to live with. And if it's hard to realize, imagine saying it aloud. For years, every time I tried to tell someone my story, I knew the moment I crossed the line in their minds. There was this look they gave me when I went there. Everyone is fine with my beliefs, and people even love the enthusiastic way I beg them to consider the medicine of needing forgiveness. But when I say aloud what I deserve, two things happen.

First, something inside my gracious friends wavers. To this point, they're tracking with me. They'll listen politely and agree that on my own, I deserve an eternity separated from my Maker. After all, the "Bible tells me so," they reason. But no one deserves a broken marriage. No one deserves infidelity. And part of me agrees. The other part of me, though, *knows*.

The other thing that happens is the logical conclusion that takes root behind the eyes. "If Meg is saying *she* deserves the pain of a relationship with a wayward husband, then she probably thinks *I do, too*. And other wives, too. And she may even believe women in abusive relationships deserve that fate, too, and that's just crazy talk." And, of course, they're right. They're right because there's something inside all of us that recognizes a human is a valuable, precious, delicate thing. And abuse is the opposite of the care merited inherently.

Believe it or not, these two stoppers kept me from writing and publishing my story for six years.

Remember, all the scriptures I'd been taught about the human condition told me that I deserved hell. In other words, if ever I've done anything wrong (hello, chapters 1, 2, and 3 of this story), then my punishment was an eternity apart from my Creator. Hell—you know, darkness, flames, torment, loneliness, and despair. Forever.

Call me crazy, but I believe in a just God who can only be with righteousness. He can't be with the unatoned me, even if He wants to. He can't stand what I've done—not because my sins are *so bad*, but because of *how good* He is. So I knew that it was grace that kept me from eternal hell, not anything I'd done well or right. And I was always grateful.

Until I started going through hell on earth.

It felt worse than flames or torment or whatever—betrayal in marriage is the worst. And so is physical and emotional abuse. And what about my friend whose little kid is going through pediatric brain cancer? That's hell. What do you do with the freak car accidents or hurricanes or dictators that devastate lives? It's hell on earth. My point is we can nod our heads in church when Preacher Man tells us what we deserve *after* this life, but *during* it? No one should ever suggest we deserve any of this suffering. It's too real. It's too raw. Right?

Wrong.

I believe we deserve it all. The small crimes we've committed against each other are big enough to merit the hell we go through on earth. Why then, does something deep within us say that's lunacy? That a battered woman should get out?

Here's why. First, because we didn't *cause* it. We may deserve it, but we didn't cause the pain.

More importantly, though, because something inside us knows that Someone has already gone through this suffering on our behalf. We shouldn't have to do it again.

God's son Jesus was beaten. He was insulted. He was betrayed. He was killed in the most painful way humanly possible so that

I don't have to go through any of what I deserve. He lived a perfect, sinless life and died the ugliest imaginable death so that if I hide under His righteousness, I am forgiven and my debt is paid. Suddenly, if I believe in His debt payment on my behalf, I'm free from what I deserve. And when I rely on that for my merit, I don't anymore deserve an unfaithful husband than my neighbor deserves the tornado that hit her home. To be clear, in Christ, the refugee now deserves safe (luxury, first-class) passage home, the fatherless kid now deserves his favorite biological male role model, and the worried mom deserves a healthy, happy child.

In short, it is wrong to suffer when Someone else has already done it for you. And this answers the "how." How does one approach a perpetrator and apologize? How do I feel grateful for my sad situation? From the never-ending gratitude that springs up when you realize what, exactly, you deserve on your own.

If the scriptures are true, then I don't just deserve the perverted husband, I also deserve an unjust earthly ruler, a chronic medical condition, the heartache of self-destructive children, and an earthquake to take my beloved home right now. For too long, we have associated hell with distant concepts like flames and torment and wondered where God is when this *life* hurts. All the while, God is every moment keeping us from what we deserve—in truth.

Casting Debt

How then, shall we live?

Well, we've established two pretty crazy things already: number one, that our *goodness* deserves hell just as surely as our sins do, and that, number two, while it's true we *deserve* hell on earth, we should not need to suffer through it, since Christ already did that for us. Whew.

The last thing we need to know is that He did more than pay our debts. He also gave us the Spirit of extra. Here's what that looks like. Will Monica's dad hurt her again? Yes. Will my husband hurt me again? Yes. Will there be more debts in your life? One hundred percent, yes. Learn to recognize a debt as soon as you see it. Say to yourself, "This person hurt me, and I can pay a portion of their debt if it's worth the emotional cut to do so." Because Someone has paid your debt and left you *extra resources* to do likewise for others.

Most days Joe only owes me five silver coins. But it's still a debt, and his pockets are empty. So I choose to pay that little debt for him—not by saying, "That's okay Joe, you can pay me another time," or "No problem, I'm in control of the accounts here, so I'll just change this to a zero." No, no, that's not a paid-for debt. That's at

best a loan, and at worst, a misprint. I instead look at all of the debts *I have incurred*, and I remember my pockets are empty, too. I tell him I'm so sorry that he had to live with my deficiencies today. I acknowledge his fantasy, the wife I *could* be (without listing her attributes in detail, of course), and how I fall short.

I acknowledge my attitude of discontentment and even self-righteousness, and recognize aloud how it can't be fun for him to live with that part. In a way, I'm paying his five denarii by showing him the one hundred I owe. How? Because Someone paid my debt *and more*.

Perhaps one of the most interesting parts of our marriage is how Joe doesn't seem to care about my debts once I grieve them aloud. He assures me we're on the same side, and we can then turn to face our combined debts together and get to work putting some payments on them. Does this put us in a constant state of debt to each other?

Yes, and guess what? It's beautiful down here. You all can keep your cleanliness and good works and pious "doing our best each day" because my husband and I are together in a huge hole of debt we'll never be able to pay, and it's glorious because we're together in that hole. Also, there's another Payee involved, Someone who doesn't fudge the books to change what we owe, but who actually made a colossal payment on our behalf once. Meantime, my husband and I acknowledge our earnings: We have earned *debts* for ourselves that we will never be able to pay.

Another time, I heard Monica speak again on the same intriguing topic. She used an illustration that's more removed from our twisted adult relationships. I find hypothetical analogies to be so poignant with people because they're stories about other

characters, so listeners are free to think about the concept without directly feeling accused. Perhaps that's why Jesus's teachings are so popular, yet offensive if you apply them to yourself. We've become so very good at taking His stories, putting ourselves in the perpetrator's shoes in those stories, and then minimizing what that implies.

Anyway, the next time I heard her speak, Monica used the scenario of a teenager and his smartphone. Now if you know anything about teenagers and their phones, well, they were practically made for each other. The story goes that the teen gives his device to a friend to show it off. The friend drops it, and the thing breaks. It's messed up but still performs half of its functions. The screen is broken, and it has a couple of new glitches and quirks.

Now, someone has to pay for this brokenness, whether or not there's an apology. Don't get me wrong; apologies are cool, and I don't know if I'd survive my marriage's insane baggage if we didn't have healthy apologies flying all over the place. And Joe's sincere (and repeated) apologies are a balm to my heart. But an apology doesn't mean things are all right. *It means now we're on the same side and ready to work together to face the debt that has been created.*

The kid who dropped the phone apologizes, and the owner of the device says something super teenager-y like "Oh bro, no no worries, bro; it's all good, bro," and together they look at the smashed smartphone and run through their choices: Either the owner lives with the damage, which would be a daily inconvenience, or in other words, small payments made over time which never seem to amount to anything. Or the owner buys a new device, which would be a big upfront payment. Or the clumsy friend who dropped it pays for a new one for the guy, another big one-time payment. Or the thing

isn't used again, and the owner lives his life without this luxury, which is another form of daily payments. The phrase "someone has to pay" sounds so nasty, but it's really not.

The thing is broken, and we cannot pretend no one will sacrifice for this brokenness. Someone is going to pay. Who is it? And how will they do it? Apologies from offenders (whether clumsy or malignant) are great, but who will pay up for the debt? However, when the phone's owner realizes that Someone already paid for the offense, he can incur the debt on behalf of his buddy without holding a grudge or hoping the cost is paid back. Now, only a teenager who's aware of his own debts (paid in full by a third Party) has, not the power, but the perspective to be able to forgive like that.

This also means that when I find a tool in my shed that I had borrowed from a friend years ago (and forgot to return), I'm not "making it right" by merely giving it back. That's not a debt paid in full. It would be wise to recognize that the friend who has been living without that thing for years has been paying on that debt since the day I borrowed it. Her living without it is a form of paying. Remember, when something is taken or broken, someone always pays for it to be made right.

We can't pretend everything's cool when it's not. Payments can look different, but someone has to do it, even if they don't agree to it. My friend was paying a little on my debt every day (by not having her garden tool), but she didn't agree to that arrangement or payment method. After all, the debt wasn't hers to begin with. So when I return the item, I can't just make it right by giving it back and saying, "I'm sorry," even if I'm sincere. This is also why, when your porn-addicted

husband apologizes, even sincerely, you will still be hurt. This is what debt feels like. And this is what it is to pay his debt for him.

Living without a garden tool may be a miniscule inconvenience in your mind, but you're not the judge of what's a big or little debt. So sure, you may think, "Chill out, lady," about the concept of daily life without a tool being a form of daily payments. In the same way, my husband was completely floored by how upset I was regarding a few stray clicks and fantasies that he had indulged. The concepts of the broken phone and borrowed tool are simply ways of bringing a hot-button, emotionally charged issue down to earth.

Something in me knew there was more to forgiveness than saying, "I forgive you." When a guy cheats, someone has to pay to make it completely right. It's not like he can uncheat, and even if he apologizes and rebuilds trust over time, that innocence and hope is lost.

So again, when men cheat, someone simply *has* to pay. And here's the thing: the men can't pay up. They can apologize, just like the clumsy teenager who broke his friend's phone, and you can say "I forgive you," and sincerely mean it, but living with the hurt is paying for his sins, just like living without a phone is paying for someone else's accidental dropping of it. So it's never made well— *unless* there's a complete change of perspective. Recognizing what you truly deserve can provide exactly that.

So when men betray their wives, someone has to "die," in Monica's words. And we women usually do it. Either by becoming bitter, old, sad shells of ourselves, letting the destruction run its course or by sacrificing our rightness on the altar where it belongs. The truth is we will pay his debt either way. Either in small payments for the rest of our lives, as we are hit anew with the realization that

he wants sex with others (and I know that's a terrible glossing over of the root thing going on with men, but really?) or we do it in a huge, conscious payment by joining him in the hole. Not erasing his debt on paper, but by taking the only thing we have of value—our rightness—and giving it toward his balance.

I'm not talking about saying, "I'm sorry I said critical things." I'm talking about acknowledging he can be every bit as smashed up as I am—all because of my believing my sins were smaller. I'm talking about telling him I know about his shame and saying aloud that I have the same thing in a different—even worse—form: pride. And the cost of that pride is hell. In other words, *betrayal,* which is hell. You see, I often hear that it's shame that keeps men in their cycle of porn use, and sure, that's a dark thing to consider, but even darker and scarier to me is my pride and indignation keeping me in a cycle of hurting someone else.

One last thought regarding the concept of "someone has to pay": even after the apology, you can say "Jesus paid it all," but He didn't. He only cleared my husband of the debt owed to Providence. He didn't pay the debt owed to me. The hurt remained. And for years, I was paying dude's debt against my will. But then one day, God showed me how much I owed by simply being me, and a rush of insight and gratitude flooded my mind and heart. The new perspective is an overflowing, always productive well of forgiveness which I pass straight on to my guy.

Return with me to the round-table discussion where the tired-looking woman told us proudly how she had told her ex-husband those three oh-so-impossible words: "I forgive you."

I knew that was the sound of a self-righteous person. On the other hand, the words of a betrayed wife who (out of the abundance of her own received forgiveness) has agreed to pay his debt to make things right sound more like this: "I'm sorry for my contribution to our problems. I know now that I believed I was cleaner than you, and that belief is toxic to you. I was so wrong."

Not fair, you say? I agree, it's not fair. In fact, it's unjust. It's kind of sick. We shouldn't have to pay the debt which our husbands incurred, even if we weren't sinless in the marriage. We should be responsible for *our* sins, not ours *and* his! But someone has to *live with the loss*. If you still think he needs to do something to pay, then obviously the debt isn't completely cancelled. It's *we* who need to pay for his debt, and we can only do it when we realize how much we've been cleared.

I still fear my husband's infidelity. And you know what? I know he still fears my critical spirit. He fears that I'm right in my negative assessments of him. But we live with that small amount of discomfort for the sake of the other's debts. That is to say, when I wonder what he's been doing online, I ask him and he answers, but naturally I still doubt him. Instead of allowing that doubt to turn into suspicion or criticism on my part, I swallow it, and the pain that swallowing it inflicts reminds me that I'm paying his debt for him, and it's an honor because I can't pay my own. Likewise, when he mistrusts my motives, he swallows that mistrust and if it feels like razors going down, he knows that the pain is a form of payment on my behalf. And he's grateful for his ability to pay my debt for me because he cannot pay his own.

Just today I was telling him how to do something, and he said, "You got it. This is a no-nag zone. I know you're not nagging, you're just trying to get some help with this household task, so I won't choose to hear criticism." Obviously, he's fighting for me by deliberately choosing to assume the best of me. He's paying my debt little by little. After all, I dig a hole of debt when I think I'm helping him but am really nagging him, and someone's got to dig us out. I can't do it. Just like the servant who owed way more than he could pay, I owe Joe more than I can pay every time I nag him. If things were fair, I and my children would be sold into slavery to pay for that debt. So I agree, it's *not* fair. If it were fair, we'd all be in *literal* chains. I'm so thankful, then, that indeed it is not fair, but that instead of justice, I am receiving mercy, as Someone else is paying my debt.

Now, if you're still with me, there's one more final implication of the ongoing debt analogy. If I'm open to the concept that I've been inflicting as much damage on my husband with my general "helping" attitude as he inflicted on me with his wandering loyalties, then apologizing will be a beautiful start, but it won't pay the debt. If I agreed earlier that my friend has been paying a little bit toward my debt each week when she couldn't use her garden tool because I still had it, well then I should also agree here that my husband has already been paying a form of payment on my colossal debt as we have gone about our dysfunctional lives, *long before I saw the damage I was doing and asked for forgiveness.*

Not only do I need to apologize for accidentally breaking his favorite thing (probably his masculinity or dignity), I also need to commit to making payments on that debt, try to avoid incurring more, and thank him for the payments he's made on my behalf, since

this really is a debt I cannot pay back even if I spent my whole life trying. Finally, I need to pay daily payments on the debt that *he* incurred by being such a weirdo online.

Last night I was getting ready for bed, and I told Joe (who starts new projects all the time) that if he wanted to keep a stupid back-yard chicken flock, well then he needs to keep them watered and fed because they're starving out there and the neighbors are wondering what kind of hillbilly place this is. I may have been logical, I may have been "right," and I may have had a good point. But the same good Friend who paid my debt whispered my words back to me, and I heard my own voice saying, "Joe, you owe me a silver coin."

Benefit of the Debt

This whole message is going to be a huge downer to people who don't "get it." The "it" is that there's unequalled joy and freedom in being absolved of a *huge* debt, and if you never realize how huge your debt is, then yeah, you're going to be miserable, constantly choking the nearest fellow servant—or reading self-help books that try to tackle the issue by requiring more effort from you.

I believe that the perspective of freedom I've been given is a no-strings-attached gift from a generous God, not something you can will yourself to have or even work toward.

I have a friend who revealed to me that repentance is a gift. And if you are living your life oblivious to the pain you're responsible for, and you're holding others accountable for their debts to *you,* well then torture is in your future, and you bet your bottom silver coin that the truth revealed would be a huge gift. Especially if it saved you from the torture that you deserve for all of these wounds you're responsible for. Especially if the "Master" in that story was willing to forgive you for both your original debt and for your ill treatment of others who owe you.

My friend says God offers the gift of repentance to those who are desperate, not those who think they can work toward it. Weird

but cool. And yeah, it's the best way I've found to explain what I have. It's a gift of repentance. Not anything I deserve—or could ever earn. These terms "undeserved" and "could never earn" are phrases I've heard before when applied to salvation, not repentance. So it's a novel, complicated thing to me that I will continue to try to explain.

Online at benefitofthedebt.com, I'll try to show what goodness this gift of repentance has brought to me and my family. I'll show more *encouraging* ways to look at the main concept (you're welcome), as well as things I would never have appreciated on display in others before, and stories of hope that would otherwise have been tension points. Join me. Seeing other captives freed is like knowing you won't be at an amusement park all alone. In the same way we are delivered of the "hell on earth" scenario we deserve, God has given us a "heaven on earth" potential if only we cling to His once-and-for-all payment that obliterates all sin, all human goodness, and leaves a little extra for us to do likewise for one another.